Gilded Craving

GILDED CRAVING

The Cowboy Justice Association:
Serials and Stalkers
Book Three

By Olivia Jaymes

www.OliviaJaymes.com

GILDED CRAVING

Copyright © 2020 by Olivia Jaymes

CHAPTER ONE

RYAN BECK LOVED his family – his sister, his mother, his father. Hell, he even loved the current family dog, a laidback mutt named Chance that his mother had rescued from a shelter.

But loving his family didn't mean that he wasn't aware that he and his parents were extremely different people. They were a million miles apart in their worldviews so he'd always found it best to spend as little time as possible with them now that he was an adult. For the most part he managed fine, limiting contact to Christmas and maybe the Fourth of July.

His younger sister Liza, on the other hand, he loved spending time with, but as grown-ups with busy lives they didn't get to hang out with one another very often. It didn't help that they lived in different states. Even finding time for a chat on the phone was difficult, which was why he was talking to her during a regular workday on the way to question a witness. His friend and work partner Luke Brewster was driving the car and playing with the radio, trying to give Ryan a bit of privacy, which was basically impossible in the enclosed space.

1

"I just don't think that I can make it," Ryan said, juggling his phone and a paper cup filled with scalding hot coffee. He hadn't slept well the night before but that wasn't anything new. "I'll send a nice gift."

Liza had told him that she was throwing a huge party for his mother's sixtieth birthday, and of course, she wanted him there.

"What's your excuse this time?" Liza challenged, impatience in her tone. "Work? A last-minute colonoscopy? Drug rehab? Your excuses are getting increasingly lame every time, big brother."

Had Ryan's excuses become more unbelievable? He'd put some time into thinking of them but his sister had caught him off guard this morning. He'd have to do better going forward. Liza was too smart for any of his half-assed efforts.

"I'm very busy," he explained. "There's always a crime to be solved and bad guys to put behind bars."

"Then they can wait one night," Liza replied promptly. "They'll be there when you get back."

"I really–"

"Don't even go there. I'm tired of all of this. I get it. You and Dad argue. Mom makes you feel guilty. Whatever. They're our parents and it's Mom's damn birthday. So you're going to be there or I'll hire two big thugs to kidnap your ass and drag you here. And you know I'll do it too, so just deal with it."

It was much more than arguing and feeling guilty. Of all people in the world, Liza should understand that. She'd been a witness to most of it.

"You know it's not that easy."

"I know that you're a grown ass man," she shot back. "But you're not acting like it. The very definition of adulthood is doing shit you don't want to do. I'm sure it's easier to ignore your family, but is that who you really want to be?"

He really didn't want to go. Every time he was home, he argued with his parents. They hated his job and almost everything else about his life. If his dad had his way, Ryan would have done exactly as he was told and lived by the Beck family rules.

I wasn't going to do that. Ever.

"I may be a grownup but I don't get treated that way when I go home," he replied defensively. "Mom and Dad act like I'm a child that doesn't know not to play in traffic."

"Just ignore it. That's what I do. You take everything far too personally, Ryan. That's the way our parents are and they aren't going to change. Were you planning to never see them again?"

No...but he'd been hoping for far bigger chunks of time between visits. The fact was it made him crazy to have to admit that this was one conundrum that he couldn't solve.

The Mystery of the Beck Family Craptastic Attitude. Why couldn't Jack and Patricia Beck respect his decisions and butt out of his life?

"Of course not, but I do have a demanding career, Liza. I can't just fly off whenever I want to. People depend on me."

"I'm depending on you too. I want you to be there at the party and make a toast for Mom's birthday. I don't want to pull the guilt card here but you have to know without me saying it out loud that Mom would be heartbroken if you weren't there."

It really all came down to that. Hadn't he always known how this phone call was going to end? He wasn't a bad son, per se. Yes, he was a disappointment to his parents but he hadn't ended up in prison or rehab.

He didn't want his mother to be sad or even worse…cry.

"I'll see what I can do about my schedule," he finally said. "But I can't make any promises."

"You'll be there," Liza replied confidently. "I know my brother and you'll make it happen. This is important, Ryan."

"You only think you know me."

Liza thought she knew everything. Or at least she had when they were kids. For the youngest in the family, she'd been quite the know-it-all.

"I have to go," she said. "I'm having lunch with Mariah."

Mariah Campbell. His sister didn't have to say the last name. In Ryan's world, there was *only one* Mariah. His fingers tightened on the cell phone in his hand, the knuckles turning white. His good mood was rapidly dissolving from this conversation. Liza knew where to hit him.

Right in the heart.

She meant well. She'd never given up on Ryan and Mariah as a couple. He had, though, long ago, but that didn't mean he'd forgotten. How could he? At one point in his life she'd been the most important thing in the world.

"Good for you. I don't need to know anything about it or her."

"But you want to, right? I don't think she's dating anyone."

Mariah had never lacked for male companionship if she wanted it. If she was single, it was by choice.

"Once again, good for Mariah. Now I have to go. I'm supposed to be working. Talk to you soon."

He hung up before Liza had another chance to fill him in on his ex-girlfriend's life news. He didn't need to know because he didn't care. She was the past. His career was the present and future.

"So you're going to a birthday party?" Luke asked, glancing in Ryan's direction and then returning his eyes to the road. "Your mom?"

"My mother's sixtieth and it's rude to listen in to other people's conversations."

Ryan was just busting Luke's balls. He didn't care that his friend had overheard.

"Excuse the hell out of me," Luke joked back. "It was hard not to hear unless I wanted to drive from the hood of the car."

A mental image of Luke doing just that had Ryan chuckling.

"I was only giving you a hard time. That was my sister Liza and she wants me to attend my mother's birthday party."

"And you don't want to?"

Ryan's friend was aware that he had issues with his family, he just didn't know what those issues were.

"It's...complicated."

Luke glanced at him again. "Okay, I won't pry. It's none of my business anyway. Now, do you want to tell me who Mariah

5

is? Because I've never heard her name before. Is she someone from your murky past?"

Ryan didn't even know where to begin when it came to Mariah.

"Mariah and I dated on and off for a long time," he finally replied. "Then we broke up. It's been years now. She got married eventually but I heard they divorced. Liza won't give it up, though. She's constantly trying to talk to me about Mariah and tell me the latest going on in her life. They're best friends and Liza always wanted them to be sisters."

"But you're not the marrying type?"

"Something like that."

"So you'll see this Mariah when you go home for the party?"

Absolutely. Ryan's parents adored her as if she was one of their own children.

"Yes, but it's not the big deal that Liza makes it out to be. It was all a long time ago. I doubt Mariah even thinks about me anymore."

"No shrine to her first love?" Luke chuckled.

"Hardly. She's not the shrine type."

"What about you? You don't spend evenings paging through your old yearbook thinking about what might have been?"

"I don't even know where my yearbooks are. Mariah's a wonderful person but she and I never could have made it work. We're far too different."

"I guess Liza is destined to be disappointed then."

"I guess she is. She's a big girl. She'll get over it. I'm not ever getting back together with Mariah."

Luke didn't reply to Ryan's declaration, instead parking the car in front of a bungalow on a residential street. They were supposed to try and speak to a witness from a cold case they were both working on. The murder had happened twenty years ago and this witness had been able to give a vague description to the cops but the killer had never been found. They were hoping that the witness might be able to tell them more information than was in the case file. As with so many cold cases, the notes and some of the other reports had been lost or misplaced.

Darren Campo was the man they were looking for and hopefully he lived here. According to their research, he lived at this address with a girlfriend. He worked nights as a security guard and according to the girlfriend he would be willing to talk to them after his shift. If they'd time this correctly, Campo would have returned home about thirty minutes ago.

Luke knocked and the door swung open revealing a middle-aged woman around forty or so. Ryan was bad at guessing ages. She might be younger but she had that world-weary expression that said that she hadn't had a good night's sleep worry-free in a long time.

"You must be the detectives that called yesterday."

Ryan pulled out a business card from his breast pocket. "Investigators, actually. We're helping the police with a cold case. I'm Ryan Beck and this is my associate Luke Brewster. Is your partner home? We'd like to talk to him."

She accepted the card and stepped back. "He is. He just got

home and he's in the kitchen eating breakfast. I'll tell him you're here."

They waited in the foyer for the woman to return. She was only gone for a few moments and then she was back beckoning them to move farther into the house.

"He's right this way. Come on in."

They followed her to the kitchen at the back of the house but no one was there. On the small table there was a half-eaten plate of food. The coffee was still steaming in the cup. The woman frowned and looked around.

"He was just here a moment ago…"

Ryan had an inkling. "Ma'am, when we called yesterday did you tell him that we were coming?"

She shook her head. "No, I didn't think he'd mind."

The sound of an engine firing up had Ryan and Luke heading back to the front door. A sedan shot out of the driveway and into the street, tires squealing.

"Shit," Ryan mumbled under his breath. "Let's go."

Luke was already on his way with Ryan on his heels. They jumped into their car and then remembered that they weren't cops anymore. They couldn't go on a high-speed chase. Ryan could only call it in to the local cops.

They were dead in the water.

"Fuck," Luke said. "Just…fuck."

That pretty much summed up the situation.

"I have a feeling that Darren Campo might not be the innocent witness and bystander that we thought he was," Ryan observed. "In a way, we got lucky. If his girlfriend had told him last night that we were coming here he'd probably be out of the state by now."

They might have broken open the case.

"Let's call the local police and then get back to the office," Luke said. "We need to let Reed know what's going on."

Ryan also needed to ask for some time off for his mother's birthday party. He didn't want to go but this was one family obligation he couldn't say no to.

And not one good thing was going to come from it.

CHAPTER TWO

R YAN WAS SITTING at his desk a few hours later when his boss Logan Wright stuck his head out of his office.

"Beck, do you have a minute?"

Closing the file he'd been perusing, Ryan picked up his can of soda. "Sure thing. I'll be right there."

Luke looked up from his laptop. "When you're done, do you want to get some lunch? Chris and Knox said that they're thinking of that barbecue place that has the great garlic toast."

"Sounds good. I'm starving. I doubt this will take long."

Logan wasn't a long-winded sort of person. Ryan would probably be in and out fairly quickly. The door to the office was open so he stepped in and settled into the chair across from his boss's desk. To his surprise, Logan stood up and closed the door behind them. Was this something that the rest of the office couldn't hear? Shit, was he being fired?

"I closed the door because I didn't want anyone to interrupt us," Logan said, reading Ryan's mind. His boss was spooky like that, always two steps ahead of anyone else. He could only hope to be half the lawman someday that Logan Wright was. "I'm sure you haven't heard yet because there hasn't been an announcement to the public, but a body was found in Chicago. An old building was being torn down and that's when they found it. The identification process took a little while due to decomposition but it's done now – Bradley Harrington, twenty-one years old."

Ryan was thirty-four but with one mention of that name he was a teenager again. He and Brad had grown up together, their families life-long friends. At the end, they hadn't been best buddies but they'd run in the same crowd, going to the same parties, and hanging out at the same places.

"Brad? Are they…sure?"

It seemed impossible. It had been thirteen years ago.

"They're sure," Logan replied, handing over a manila file folder. "The identification details are in here along with the information about the area where they found the body."

Numbly, Ryan accepted the file but didn't open it. He was still stunned, to be honest. After so many years, he'd been sure that they would never find out what happened to Brad.

"You knew Bradley Harrington," Logan said when Ryan didn't respond. "You were friends?"

"Kind of. We were good friends when we were kids but you know how it is as you get older. We went to different colleges and sort of grew apart. We had the same friend group, though, so during holidays and summers we would all get together." Ryan shook his head. "Sorry about this. I'm just…blown away. It's been years and we never heard anything else after about six months from when he disappeared."

"What do you remember about the case?"

That it had almost been too bizarre to be real. Even now it sounded like something out of a movie or book.

"We were all partying that night, bar hopping and generally being wild-ass kids. We'd all finished our junior year and we hadn't been home long. A few weeks? I remember thinking that I shouldn't stay out too late because I had a flight out of O'Hare at noon the next day. We all did, actually. We were going to celebrate the end of the school year with a vacation in Hawaii."

"Is that what you did? Go home early?"

Ryan grimaced at the memory. He and Mariah had almost missed their flight. They'd made it by the skin of their teeth.

"Not as early as I should have. We overslept the next morning but made it."

"And Brad wasn't there?"

Logan obviously had more information about the case than he'd let on in the beginning of this conversation.

"No, but we weren't worried. We figured he'd overslept like we did and missed the flight. We assumed he'd be on the next one."

"But that didn't happen."

"He never made it to Hawaii."

Even then Ryan and his friends hadn't been all that concerned. Brad had always been a wild one, doing his own thing. It wouldn't have surprised any of them if he'd met up with someone and spent the week drinking and partying. To Brad there was no such thing as a stranger; he made friends wherever he went. Ryan had tried to call him several times and there was no answer, but they'd all laughed and said that Brad must be having one hell of a time not to pick up his phone.

"When was the last time you saw him alive?"

Swallowing hard, Ryan rubbed at his chin. "At the bar. We were doing shots."

"From the police report that was the last time anyone saw him. The security cameras showed him entering the bar but never leaving it." Logan pointed to the file folder still in Ryan's hand. "They found the body in the lot next to that bar. It had been under construction at the time of his disappearance. The police theory is that your friend got drunk, stumbled out the back door, and fell into a hole or ditch."

Already shaking his head, Ryan finally opened the folder. "That couldn't have happened. The back exit was one of those fire doors. If anyone opened it an alarm went off. A loud one. Ask me how I know. He couldn't have gone out that way without everyone knowing. As for that lot, it was under construction but there weren't any holes or ditches that I remember. They were almost done with the building."

"It's just a theory at this point. The investigation is ongoing." Logan sat back in his chair, his gaze intent on Ryan. "May I ask what you thought happened to him?"

"You can but I'm not sure that I have a simple answer. For a long time after Brad's disappearance we all had various theories. A few even thought that he might have been trying to fake his own death and start a new life. He'd actually talked about that once but I'm sure he was just bullshitting like we always did. He wasn't going to walk away from family and friends. He was – in current terms – living his best life, if you know what I mean. The guy was having a ball and with his family's connections his future was golden. I can't imagine that he'd want to throw all that away. No, I always assumed that he'd trusted the wrong person and got himself hurt. As wild as Brad was, he was always a little naive and trusting. He'd lived a sheltered life to a certain extent."

"As did you, I would imagine."

Ryan had always assumed that Logan, Jason, and Jared knew all about his family. They'd never said anything out loud but they knew how often a suspect ordered pizza and what Netflix shows they liked to watch. It wasn't a far stretch to assume that they also knew that Ryan came from big family money and had grown up privileged and wealthy.

"You could say that I did," Ryan conceded. "Not from choice, though."

"So what do you think about this?"

"I'm not sure what you're asking," Ryan admitted. "I think that it's going to be difficult to find out what really happened to Brad after all of these years if that's what you mean."

"It is going to be difficult which is why the Harrington family has requested that you work on the case. They want to know for sure what happened to their son that night, and if foul play was involved, who did it."

Charles "Skip" Harrington and his wife Lily were asking for him? How did they even know where he worked?

Of course...Ryan's parents. They were close friends with Skip and Lily. They had been even before Ryan and Brad were born.

"I doubt the Chicago police want me nosing around their case," Ryan said, trying to stall while his brain whirled with this new information. He needed time to digest all of this before he responded to any requests. "We don't even know if there is case to be investigated. According to this file that you gave me, the cause of death is still pending. It might have been an accident."

Logan nodded in agreement. "And if it is the parents still want to know how it happened. If it's not...they want to know who is responsible and have them brought to justice. Apparently, the family has a theory about a serial killer that was operating in Chicago at the time kidnapping college kids, murdering them, and then dumping the bodies. He was never caught. They've always felt that their son was one of his victims but the police didn't think there was enough evidence to tie it together with the other cases. As for the cops, I don't think they have any say in this. The Harrington family is well-connected, as you know, and they want a private firm brought in to assist."

"Our firm?"

"Yes, and you specifically. I have to say I think that they're right. You're the perfect person for the job. You already know the people involved in the case and you have their trust and confidence. I could send someone else but I don't think that they'll be able to do the job as quickly as you could."

"It's...but my family..."

"I also think that you might want to know what happened to your friend all those years ago," Logan said as if Ryan hadn't just spoken.

"I do want to know," he admitted. "But it's not a simple thing."

"Spending time with your family?"

"We don't have the best relationship. They don't approve of what I do or the life that I'm leading. They want me to join the family business."

"Parents can be that way." Logan turned to his laptop and tapped on the keys. "I can only guess as to your relationship with your family so I'm going to leave it up to you. If you want to do it, I'll send you out right away and then Luke can join you to help when we free him up here. If you don't want to go, I understand. We'll assign someone else. If I give you the night to think it over, can you give me your answer first thing in the morning?"

"I can."

He'd know what he wanted to do by then, right? All of his instincts were telling him to run far away from this case, but there was a part deep inside that wanted answers. Logan was right about one thing. Ryan already knew Brad's friends and family. He knew Brad. That was a huge advantage that another investigator wouldn't have.

If only he could do the job without having to go home.

★ ★ ★

MARIAH TOOK A sip of whiskey, letting the burn go all the way to her belly. She and her best friend Liza had just toasted an old friend who had died. Actually, he'd died many years ago when they were all in college but they hadn't found out for sure until today. His body had been found when they'd torn down an old building next to one of the bars they'd all frequented at the time.

"Brad was a good guy," Liza said with a sad sigh. "At least now his parents will know what happened to him. It has to have been terrible all these years left wondering what happened to their son."

"I can't even imagine it," Mariah replied with a shake of her head. So many memories of happier times were running through her mind. They'd all been so young and carefree back then. It was a lifetime ago. "I hope this gives them some sort of peace."

Liza picked up her cell phone from the coffee table between them. They were drinking mid-afternoon in Mariah's apartment after having lunch together downtown. "Maybe I should call Ryan and tell him the news."

Mariah inwardly flinched but hoped her expression gave nothing away. She hadn't seen Ryan Beck in years, the last time at Liza's wedding five years ago.

"I'm sure he's going to come for Mom's birthday party. I told him he didn't have any excuse and that he'd better be there."

Mariah didn't even try to fool herself that it would be easy to see him. Sadly, they'd gone in different directions as they'd grown up mostly because he wouldn't compromise one iota. Ryan Beck was a stubborn jackass but he'd also been more than a boyfriend at one time. He'd been her best friend. Even now, she keenly felt his loss in her life. He was a man that was difficult to get over.

"I assumed he'd be there," Mariah replied, taking another sip of whiskey. "You should call him. He'd want to know about Brad."

"They weren't the best of friends at the end. Didn't he punch Brad in the nose when he got too close to you?"

At a party. The whole group had been there.

"I handled Brad on my own. I didn't need Ryan to fight my battles for me."

Even though he'd wanted to punch Brad. A whole bunch.

"He loved you a lot back then. You loved him too."

"Where are you going with this?" Mariah asked with a heavy sigh. "Because your brother and I broke up a long time ago and we're not going to get back together. Give up on that fantasy."

Liza made a face and then took a drink from her highball glass. "They say a first love never dies."

Mariah didn't want to believe that.

"They also say that a first love is just a rehearsal, a practice run for the real thing. I loved Ryan but we were both kids then. I hope that I'm grown up enough to realize that love isn't always enough."

Liza nodded sympathetically. "He's my brother and I love

him but he can be a piece of work. All of his talk about not wanting to live like Mom and Dad or be like them. He wanted to make a name for himself on his own and all that jazz. I get it and all but you're right. He's so fucking militant about it. It gets on my nerves."

"He has a point, though," Mariah said. "He wants to be his own man and I respect that."

Liza's smile widened. "I think that maybe you have the patience for him after all."

"I said I respect it, not that I want a daily dose of it."

Liza laughed at Mariah's statement. "You have to admit that my brother won the gene pool lottery. He's still handsome as hell."

Ryan Beck had been completely and totally gorgeous when she'd known him. And he didn't care about his looks at all. She assumed he was still the same way.

"I wouldn't know. I haven't seen him in years, remember?"

Liza held up her phone. "I can show you a photo. I have one I took at Christmas."

Mariah thought it better to ignore the offer. She wanted to see it but it probably wouldn't be a good idea. With the news about Brad today, she'd already be thinking about the past far too much.

"I feel like we should do something," Mariah said, emptying her whiskey glass. She wanted another, to be honest. "But I don't know what."

Normally when someone died she'd send flowers to the funeral, but she didn't have any idea what the Harringtons were going to do. They'd never had a memorial service when Brad disappeared because they'd always held out hope that he would be found alive.

"That's how situations like this make you feel. Helpless."

Mariah didn't like that feeling one bit. She'd always prided herself on having control of her life. Was she simply fooling herself? Maybe no one had any control. Brad hadn't that night so long ago.

They'd all been together that evening, laughing and having fun. Then...*something* had happened. Something awful.

Funny how a person can think that they left their past far behind them, but the universe always had other plans. She'd be thinking about Brad and Ryan today. She'd be thinking about the girl she once was.

And what might have been. That was the most painful part of all.

CHAPTER THREE

R YAN WENT TO lunch with the other guys on the taskforce – Luke, Chris Marks, and Knox Owens. As usual, they'd ended up at their favorite sports bar. The food was good, the prices reasonable, and the service friendly. The atmosphere was generally loud and boisterous with darts, pool tables, and about a dozen television screens all around the restaurant. No one was going to overhear them talk about a grisly murder or a bloody crime scene.

He ordered a greasy cheeseburger, extra crispy fries, and a soda. He'd work it off in the gym tomorrow morning, but in truth, he'd been born lucky with a fast metabolism. He could indulge now and then and today he didn't want grilled salmon with a side of broccoli. He'd only ever met one other person who could burn off their food faster than he could.

Mariah.

Nope. He wasn't going to do this. He had more important topics to think about. He had a decision to make.

Knox elbowed Ryan. "So what did Logan call you into his office about? Is it a new case?"

Three sets of curious eyes were looking at Ryan, waiting for his answer. What the hell...he might as well tell them. They'd find out eventually.

"It is," he confirmed, weighing his words carefully. He'd grown incredibly close to these three guys in the last year. Perhaps it was time to reveal a little more about himself. The men weren't the type to judge him. "When I was in college, a friend of mine disappeared and was never found. We assumed that he'd died but of course we didn't know anything for sure. Turns out his body was found in a construction site in Chicago a few days ago. His family wants me to look into the circumstances of his death and disappearance."

Luke's brows rose. "So when do you fly out?"

"That's the thing. I'm not sure that I want the assignment. I'm supposed to think it over tonight and let Logan know tomorrow."

There was silence as if they were mulling over his answer. It was unusual for any of them to get to decide what they worked on. If they were assigned, *they were assigned.*

"Is there a reason that you wouldn't work on this?" Chris finally asked, glancing around the table. "It sounds right up our team's alley."

Now was the time. Bite the bullet and just do it.

"I've never really talked about my family much but we don't really get along. They didn't want me to become a cop. They wanted me to go into the family business."

"What is the family business?" Knox asked.

"Investments. Hedge funds. Real estate. Wall Street, basically."

Luke stroked his chin. "Sounds…lucrative."

"It is," Ryan sighed. "I don't really like talking about my family, to be honest. I'm close to my sister but my parents think I'm a failure and that they raised me wrong."

"So they have money?" Knox queried. "They're rich?"

"Old money. The kind that has passed through generations," Ryan confirmed. "And I'm the son that broke the tradition. You can imagine how popular that makes me at Thanksgiving."

Luke whistled and shook his head. "I can see where that might ruffle a few feathers. We all had figured out that you had some tension with your folks, and we weren't going to pry in your personal business. I can understand how this case might be awkward for you."

"So that means you're rich," Knox said with a chuckle. "Did you think we'd stick you with the dinner check every time if we knew?"

"No, but it's a weird topic," Ryan admitted. "Some people are very put off by it. I don't live in a mansion or anything. I'm just like everybody else."

His friends exchanged glances, smiles playing on their lips.

"Not quite like everybody," Chris piped up, a grin spreading across his face. "That truck you drive is a limited edition with every bell and whistle that the dealership offers. It probably cost what my condo did."

"It's just a truck," Ryan protested, shaking his head. "It's utilitarian."

Knox pointed to Ryan's shoes. "And those? They cost at least a month's salary, and don't argue with me about it. I know my boots and shoes. I worked in a men's clothing department while I was in school. Let's face it, friend. We've all noticed that you have expensive shit but we weren't going to say anything about it."

His mouth open, Ryan didn't know what to say. They'd noticed?

"Why didn't you say anything?"

"Because it was none of our business," Chris replied quietly. "It still isn't. But yes, we noticed that you had a little extra cash here and there for clothes and trips and such. We wouldn't be very good investigators if we hadn't noticed, now would we?"

"Were you ever tempted to check out my finances?" Ryan asked.

He had to know the truth.

"No," Luke said firmly. "It was your damn business. I always assumed that eventually you might say something if the subject came up but frankly, the last thing I want to talk about is someone else's money. I was brought up to never mention it and I plan to stick to that."

The other guys nodded in agreement. Here Ryan had thought he was fooling everyone, but apparently he wasn't as average as he'd thought he was.

"I'm just like everyone else," he said again. "I'm not any different."

"Sure, you're one of the guys," Luke agreed, slapping Ryan on the back. "Nobody thinks of you any differently. Now tell us about this case because if you don't want to do it, I might want to."

"Me too," Chris said.

"I have to agree," Knox replied as well. "It sounds interesting."

Over their meal Ryan filled them in on what he knew, which wasn't much. They didn't even have a cause of death yet.

"So he walked into a bar and never came out?" Knox said as they finished up their meals. "And no one ever heard from him again?"

"No one," Ryan confirmed. "He was supposed to meet us at the airport the next day to catch a flight for Hawaii but he never showed. He didn't answer our calls and when we got back, we found out that no one had seen him since that night at the bar."

"His parents didn't call the police or anything?" Chris asked.

"Eventually they did when we all got back from our trip. They thought he was with us. They'd assumed that he'd gotten up early and taken a cab to the airport, which could have been the case. We didn't have any proof that he didn't go home after the bar closed down, and we didn't have any proof that he didn't go to the airport. We only know that he didn't make it to the flight. Or any of the later ones."

"Except that now he's been found in the lot next to the bar," Luke said. "So one could conclude that he never left that night."

"It's a reasonable assumption," Ryan agreed. "But there are

still unanswered questions. If it was an accident, how did it happen? If it wasn't an accident…well…that's a whole Pandora's Box, isn't it? Who did it and why?"

Chris shook his head. "And you're telling us that you're not even remotely curious as to the answers? This was your friend and you don't want to know what happened to him all those years ago?"

It wasn't that simple.

"He was my friend but we had a complicated relationship."

Knox's brows pinched together. "So you don't want to know?"

"I do want to know. I just don't want what comes with this investigation."

"Your family," Luke guessed. "You think they'll take the opportunity to give you a hard time?"

"Every chance they get. I don't think they will, I know they will."

Knox had a strange look on his face, one that Ryan had never seen before.

"You look like you have something to say."

His friend shrugged. "Not really. Except to say that I've been a disappointment to my family all my life and that wouldn't keep me from finding out what happened to an old friend. My family has their opinions about my life and I have mine."

"And you don't care what they think?"

"Not particularly," Knox said with a smile. "They couldn't convince me when I was just a kid that I was a loser, so now that

I'm a grown man I doubt that anything they say is going to sway me. I'm not that weak in my convictions."

"I'm not either."

"Okay, I was just making an observation."

Knox was always doing shit like this. Raising a question, getting everyone all riled up, and then stepping back like it was no big deal.

The thing was…no one was riled up but Ryan which meant that Knox had hit a nerve.

Am I weak in my convictions? Is that why I won't go back? Because I could be talked out of the decisions I've made?

Fuck no. I just don't want to go because my parents are a pain in the ass.

"Your observations suck," Ryan replied bluntly. "Keep them to yourself."

Knox shoved a fry in his smiling mouth. "Happy to."

Chris wagged a finger at Knox. "Just ignore him. He likes to act like he's so wise and all but he doesn't know shit."

That's exactly what Ryan was going to do. Knox couldn't possibly understand the pressure that he was under when he was around his family. They were never going to give up and let him live his life.

But he did want to know what happened to Brad. Could he risk a trip back home to find the answers? Did he dare delve into a past that was best left behind?

Then there was Mariah. She'd be there.

She was the one person he didn't think he could face.

CHAPTER FOUR

O'HARE AIRPORT HADN'T changed since the last time Ryan had flown in – just as big and perhaps even busier. He grabbed a cab to his apartment while tapping out a text to Logan to let him know that he'd arrived.

After talking with the guys at lunch, there hadn't been much left for Ryan to mull over. He was going to take the case. He wanted to know what had happened to Brad all those years ago, and he was in the perfect position to do the investigation. He knew the players and – for the most part – he had their trust.

As for Mariah, he was sure he could avoid her. He'd see her at the party but the rest of the time he'd give her a wide berth. She'd been at the bar the night that Brad had disappeared but he probably didn't even need to talk to her. He'd been with her the entire evening so her recollection was his recollection. At least that's what he was telling himself.

Chicago traffic was heavy but eventually the cab pulled up in front of his apartment building located in Lincoln Park. He'd had a hard time explaining to his firm's administrative assistant that he didn't need a hotel booked for the trip. He already had a place to stay. His parents owned the building and they'd gifted him the apartment when he'd graduated from college. They'd said they always wanted him to have a home in Chicago no matter what happened in his life. He'd taken it as they didn't think he could make a living and pay for a place to live on a cop's salary. But it did come in handy from time to time.

When he came to visit, he didn't have to stay in his parents' home or impose on his sister and brother-in-law. He could decompress in his own place and even leave his socks on the floor if he wanted to. He couldn't do that living with Jack and Patricia. They liked their home to look like no one actually lived there.

He pushed his key into the apartment door but it didn't click, simply swinging open. He could hear the sound of music and some familiar off-key singing.

Liza, his sister. What was she doing here?

"You're lucky I don't have a gun. I might have shot you."

She had his refrigerator and kitchen cabinets wide open; brown grocery bags were spread out over the marble countertops. When she saw him, she grinned and ran straight for him, wrapping him in a big hug.

"It's so good to see you," she squealed, pressing a kiss to his cheek and hugging him again. "I was hoping to have all of this done before you got here. Your flight must have made good time. And no, I don't think you would have shot me."

"I didn't expect you here. You should never surprise a cop."

"You're a former cop and I'm your sister. Besides, are you

really that jumpy that you'd shoot first and ask questions later? You might want to see someone about that if it's true."

His gaze ran over the overflowing bags. "How about you tell me what you're doing here? How did you even know that I was coming?"

Her brows rose. "Maybe I have a crystal ball?"

If she did it was Waterford.

"You've never been psychic in your life. Try again."

She heaved a sigh and rolled her eyes. He was struck by how much she resembled their mother. Long dark hair and brown eyes. Petite and slim. How had he not noticed that before? There was a photo of Patricia Beck on the fireplace mantle in their vacation home in Paris that looked just like Liza.

"You called the doorman and he called me. Simple."

"Why did the doorman call you?"

She shoved a container of ice cream into the freezer. Chocolate. He made a mental note to rip into that later tonight.

"Because I'm managing most of the family real estate these days, brother dear."

"I didn't know that."

"You would know if you took an interest in your family."

"I take an interest."

"Barely." She snapped the freezer door shut. "So anyway, the doorman told me you were coming and I decided to be a lovely sister and fill your pantry so you wouldn't starve."

He held up his phone. "I can order in."

"You could but I know you. You like to cook."

He did like to cook. Nothing was better than a home-cooked meal. He was self-taught but he wasn't too bad in the kitchen. He hadn't poisoned anyone yet, and the people he'd cooked for were quite complimentary.

"Thank you, that was nice. It looks like you bought out the store, though. I may not be here that long."

She folded up one of the empty grocery bags. "That was my next question. How long are you going to be here? Obviously, you'll be here for the party."

It was only coincidence that he'd been assigned to a case at the same time as his mother's birthday party, but yes, he would be here for that.

"Actually, I'm here in Chicago on a case."

Her head jerked up and her brows pinched together. "A case? You're not here for the party?"

"I *will* be here for the party," he stated firmly. "I promise. But I was assigned to investigate Brad's death. You probably don't know but–"

"I know," she interrupted, her lips turning down sadly. "I know about Brad. Mom mentioned that the family was going to try and get you to investigate, but to be honest I assumed you'd say no."

Ryan ignored the fact that saying no had been his first re-sponse.

"You didn't think I'd care enough?"

Liza shrugged. "I was eighteen months younger than you but I ran with the same crowd. I don't remember you and Brad being best buddies."

"We were friends...especially when we were younger."

"Time changes some things. Still, I'm glad that you said yes. I would imagine finding out what happened that night won't be easy. It was so long ago."

"What do you remember about that night?"

Softly chuckling, Liza smiled at her memories. "That I wasn't supposed to be in that bar to begin with. I had a fake ID and I was afraid to get caught. Mom and Dad would been livid if they found out. I also remember that Mike asked me to dance. I was so excited."

Mike Monroe was Liza's husband but they hadn't started dating that night. It had been several years before they'd ended up together. Ryan had always liked the guy and he'd been glad when they'd married.

"Speaking of Mike, how's he doing? I haven't talked to him in awhile."

"He's so busy," Liza explained. "He has several big cases that he's handling. I hardly see him during the week. He works crazy hours."

Mike worked for his family's law firm and was one of the leading corporate attorneys in Chicago. Maybe New York City and Los Angeles too.

"Are you going to want to talk to him?" she asked, placing the last of the groceries in the cabinets. "He was there and he was friends with Brad."

"Eventually I'll need to talk to everyone."

When Liza didn't reply right away, he knew something was up. She was rarely at a loss for words.

"Is there something you want to say?"

She tucked the garbage bags in a lower cabinet and then straightened. "I was just going to tell you that talking to Mariah won't be a problem."

He hadn't really planned on talking to Mariah, but he wasn't going to tell his sister that.

"That's good."

Liza picked up her handbag and dug into it, jangling her keys. "I didn't tell you before but I guess I better tell you now so you're not surprised. Again. I wouldn't have to tell you these things if you spent more time here with your family."

More guilt.

"You're getting almost as good as Mom when it comes to sending me on a guilt trip. Spit it out. What's going on?"

She huffed a bit but continued. "Fine. Talking to Mariah won't be a problem because she lives across the hall. She bought the other half of this floor right after Christmas. She uses it as her home and art studio. So if you were thinking about trying to avoid her, I'm afraid that won't be possible. She's your neighbor. Now I need to get going. I have an appointment in a few hours. How about we try to have lunch tomorrow? I'll let you pick up the check."

Mariah? Only a few feet away. This could not be happening.

The one woman he didn't want to see was sleeping across the hall.

This wasn't going to be good. Not for him, and probably not for her.

They just didn't belong together. End of story.

RYAN'S VOICE WAS deep and rich, like melted chocolate on the senses. It had sent tingles down Mariah's spine when they were together. She could have listened to him read the phone book and been happy as a clam. She'd teased him once that he should have been a stage actor, spouting Shakespeare for an adoring audience. He'd just laughed and not taken her seriously.

That summed up their entire relationship in a nutshell. She'd talk and he wouldn't take her seriously. He'd already made up his mind about...everything. He didn't know much about compromising and he hadn't loved her enough to try. Or maybe he simply didn't know how. She'd had her issues as well. Patience hadn't been her strong suit and she hadn't known how bad *for better or worse* could get. She did now, though. Her divorce had been final for about a year. She wasn't all that proud that she hadn't been able to make it work.

Maybe it never was Ryan at all. Maybe I was always the problem.

It had been a long time since she'd heard Ryan's voice – since Liza's wedding five years ago. She and Ryan had tried to avoid one another that day but they were both in the wedding party and it had been pretty much impossible. She'd actually seen him duck into the kitchen at the reception when she was walking in his direction. She hadn't planned to speak to him. She'd only be heading to the ladies' room.

Since it had been so long, Mariah had assumed she was immune to it. Wrong.

She'd been coming home from a meeting today, just unlocking her own front door, when she'd heard his voice. It had permeated the old walls in the building and once more she was transported back to the past. She'd been spending far too much time there since Brad's body had been discovered.

She couldn't say she wasn't warned. Liza had called and told her that Ryan was coming to Chicago for the party but Mariah had thought it wouldn't be this soon. She'd scurried into her own apartment and quickly shut the door as if she could block out the memories that always crowded her thoughts whenever Ryan was in the same city limits.

She'd dated other men. She'd even been in love with one or two of them. What was it about this *one* man that made her lose all common sense? It was almost enough to have her pouring a glass of wine in the middle of the day.

Almost.

Instead, she rummaged in her pantry and grabbed the bag of dark chocolate that she kept for emergencies. She needed a hit of sugar and she needed it quickly to bring her back to reality. It wasn't thirteen years ago. It was now, the present.

Ryan Beck was the past. That's where he needed to stay.

CHAPTER FIVE

S KIP AND LILY Harrington lived in a penthouse overlooking Lake Michigan. Ryan had been there several times in his youth and it appeared that not much had changed. The doorman was different and the carpeted hallways looked freshened up but the inside of the Harrington home was almost identical except for a few different paintings on the walls.

Their fireplace mantle had several photos of Brad through the years and Ryan found his gaze resting on them long enough that it caught the notice of Lily.

"He was such a handsome young man," Lily said, her tone full of pride for her oldest son. "I think he favors his father but he has my eyes."

Lily did have the same blue eyes.

"I think he does look like you," Ryan said, settling on the edge of a chair. Lily and Skip were sitting on the couch to his right. "He has your chin too."

That statement apparently pleased Lily because she beamed, reaching out to pat her husband's arm. "I think Ryan might be right."

Skip nodded and held his wife's hand. He wasn't smiling. "We're very grateful that you could come on such short notice and handle this investigation. I'm not sure that the police are going to give it much attention, to be honest. They seem to think that it all happened too long ago."

The Harrington family had a great deal of pull in Chicago and were well-connected, Ryan had a feeling that the police were going to do more than they normally would but they were trying to temper expectations.

I need to do that too. Right now.

"Solving a cold case isn't easy," Ryan replied. "Memories get fuzzy, witnesses disappear or pass on, and evidence gets lost. It's an uphill battle and we don't always win. I'm going to do my very best for you but you need to understand that I may not be able to find out what truly happened to Brad that night."

"If anyone can find out, it's you," Lily said. "You were there."

"I was," Ryan conceded. "But I wasn't around Brad the whole night. I don't know that I have anything to add to the investigation."

"You're a Beck," Skip said confidently, a small smile appearing on his tanned and lined face. "So I know you won't give up until you find out what happened to my boy. I have confidence in you."

A Beck? What did that even mean?

"I'll do my best for you. I just want us all to be on the same page." He cleared his throat. This part wasn't going to be easy.

Parents always think that they know everything about their child, but the reality was they rarely do. "What can you tell me about Brad that last week before he disappeared? Did he have any visitors? Was he acting strangely? Anything at all that you might be able to tell me could help, even if you think it's not important."

Lily and Skip exchanged a quick glance and through some unspoken agreement decided to let Skip start.

"Brad was in good spirits," the older man said. "He'd had a few bumps in the road during the school year but he'd pulled it together at the end of the semester and done well. He was planning on going to law school so he could join the family firm. Did he tell you that?"

"He did," Ryan confirmed. "He was hoping for Yale Law, just like you."

Skip nodded again. "It would have meant the world to me to have my son following in my footsteps."

They were silent and Ryan didn't prod, letting them gather their thoughts in their own time. He'd learned not to intervene or try to guide the conversation too much.

"He was dating Caroline." Skip fidgeted on the couch, his lips pressed together. "She ended up marrying Danny. He was Brad's best friend."

He was speaking about Caroline Charles and Daniel Bosworth. Ryan had attended their wedding about eight years ago. They appeared to be a happy couple.

Lily nudged her husband. "Skip, it wasn't like she ran off

with Danny the next day. It was years later and she deserves to be happy. After all, Brad–"

"I won't hear ill of my dead son," Skip interjected, color rising in his cheeks. "He was young and just sowing some wild oats. He wouldn't hurt anyone on purpose."

Fortunately – or maybe unfortunately – Ryan knew what Lily was referring to. He'd run in a small, rather tight knit group and everyone had known everyone else's business.

"I'm aware that Brad was seeing other girls," Ryan said. "It wasn't a huge secret. I'm sure Caro was aware as well, to be honest."

Lily's eyes were wet with unshed tears. "As Skip said, Brad was young. He would have straightened up eventually and married Caroline."

Ryan didn't want to contradict their beliefs but he'd heard Brad on more than one occasion saying that he didn't want to marry anybody until he was over forty. He'd liked his freedom and didn't want to be tied down. He'd liked Caroline too but he hadn't been all that serious about her. She was simply the girlfriend that his parents approved of. Brad kept the other females in his life away from his mom and dad.

"Do you know any of the other girls that Brad was seeing? Their names would be helpful."

Skip shook his head. "We don't but their names might be in his phone."

"Do you have his phone?"

Ryan was sure that Brad had it with him that night.

"The police recovered the phone," Lily explained, a few tears escaping down her cheeks. "It was with...him."

In other words, they'd found it with the body.

"We'd just bought him a brand-new iPhone," Skip said, his hand reaching for Lily's. "He was really excited about it."

Ryan remembered that. Smart phones had been brand new back then and they'd all wanted the latest toy. Brad had been one of the first to get his.

"I'll check with the police to get access to it."

It probably would be a waste of time though. A phone buried underground wasn't going to be in any sort of decent condition. With any luck, his firm might be able to pull information from phone records.

"If they give you any trouble, let me know. They told me they'd cooperate fully with you," Skip replied, his bushy brows pulled down. "I'll call Stan or Gary."

Stan was a congressman and Gary was a senator. Skip played golf with them regularly. So did Ryan's dad. They all belonged to the same country club.

"Is there anything else you can remember?" Ryan queried. "Was he out of sorts about anything? Secretive? Was he mad or sad or excited?"

"He was excited about the trip to Hawaii," Lily said, wiping a tear from her cheek. "He talked about it whenever we saw him."

"Did you see him that day? Was there anything unusual?"

Skip shook his head. "We didn't see him that day but that

wasn't strange or anything. He was twenty-one and he had his own life. We'd see him every few days at dinner or he'd stop by my office for a cup of coffee."

Ryan hadn't spent all that much time with his family either. He'd wanted to believe that he was all grown up. Of course, he hadn't been but he wanted to think that he was.

"We think that the serial killer did this," Skip said, urgency in this tone. "There was a serial killer then that was abducting college kids and killing them. He did this to my boy. I just know it."

"I spent the flight here reading up on that killer," Ryan replied. "We'll have to see what the coroner has to say about cause of death. That murderer had a very specific signature."

Strangulation. With a rope.

"And they never caught him," Skip said angrily, his hands tightening into fists. "He could still be out there roaming the streets and killing people."

Considering the murders had abruptly stopped, Ryan was of the opinion that the killer was incarcerated for other crimes, but he didn't go into that. The older man didn't want to hear theories from Ryan. He wanted answers.

I don't blame him. He and his wife have waited a long time.

Pulling a business card from his breast pocket, Ryan held it out to the couple. "If you think of anything else, please let me know. You can call me twenty-four hours a day. I may have other questions for you as this investigation unfolds, I hope that's all right?"

"Whatever you need," Skip said, levering to his feet, his hand still holding his wife's. Lily stood as well. "I mean that. Whatever you need, just let me know. Forensic experts, lab tests. Whatever, I'll get it for you. I want my son to rest in peace. I haven't had a decent night's sleep in over a decade."

"Thank you." Ryan stood and they moved toward the front door. "I'll keep you in the loop but don't be alarmed if you don't hear from me every day."

"That's fine."

Ryan reached for the door handle but didn't get a chance before it swung open. A man stood there and for a moment Ryan thought it was Brad. But that couldn't be because Brad was gone.

"Seb," Lily exclaimed. "I thought you were coming over for dinner tonight."

Sebastian Harrington, Brad's younger brother. He'd been a senior in high school when Ryan and his friends were juniors in college.

"I still am but I decided to come by early when my schedule opened up due to a cancellation. I have some issues for the memorial service that we need to settle."

"Seb, you remember Ryan Beck, don't you?"

His expression grim, Seb shook Ryan's hand. "I do. It's great to see you again although I'd prefer different circumstances."

"As would I."

"Since you're here I'd like to ask you a question," Ryan said. "Did you notice anything out of the ordinary with Brad in the weeks before his disappearance? Anything at all?"

The younger man shook his head. "I'm afraid I didn't. To be truthful, I barely saw him when he was back from university. I'd just come home from school and there this was this girl that I was dating... Let's just say she had my complete attention. You know how teenage boys are."

Ryan did indeed remember.

"If you think of anything let me know."

"I will. We're so grateful that you could do this, Ryan. My family deserves the truth."

Ryan bid the Harringtons goodbye with a promise to check in with them if he learned anything. Seb was right. They did deserve the truth.

But... the thing about the truth was it didn't care if it hurt a person or not. The truth had no morals, no sympathy, no mercy.

The truth about Brad might not be what they hoped for.

CHAPTER SIX

I T WAS DINNER time and Mariah hadn't felt like cooking. It wasn't that much fun to fix dinner for one person which meant she ate far too much takeout. Usually she ordered several entrees and then heated them up for the next few days. Since she worked from home and often strange hours it was more convenient to have a stock of prepared meals in her refrigerator. Tonight she'd ordered from her favorite Italian place and she could already taste the stuffed shells in sauce, smothered in mozzarella cheese.

When her friends would ask her about her love life, she often made the joke that she was in a serious relationship with the pizza delivery guy. She certainly saw him on a more regular basis than her last boyfriend. She'd found that she had much less patience for men's crap than she did when she was younger. She dated here and there but she wasn't looking for anything serious. She'd had a few dates recently with a nice man but it wasn't going to go anywhere. She could already tell.

She took a quick shower to clean off the day and put on a comfortable pair of shorts and a t-shirt that could only be described as scruffy and well-loved. There were holes at the neckline and hem but the material was so soft she couldn't bring herself to throw it out.

Switching on the television, she glanced at the clock. Her food should be arriving any minute now. She'd forgotten to eat lunch so she was starving. She was clicking through the channels trying to find something to watch when her doorbell rang. Tossing the remote aside, she padded on barefoot to the door and opened it, ready to ask Freddie how his girlfriend and cat were doing but her words stuck in her suddenly dry throat.

Freddie wasn't standing there. Ryan was. Holding a giant brown bag of delicious smelling food.

"I think this is yours," he said, holding out the sack. "It was delivered to me by accident."

It took a second for his words to penetrate her brain and for her arms to reach out and accept the food. She was careful that their hands didn't touch.

Damn, he looked good. She'd been right not to let Liza show her a recent picture. As expected, Ryan had only become more handsome since the last time she'd seen him. He was all tall, dark, and gorgeous.

"Freddie delivered this to you?"

It didn't make any sense. She and the delivery guy were on a first name basis. She knew the name of his cat, for heaven's sake.

Hercules, by the way.

But Ryan's sudden appearance had her all in a tizzy, so it wasn't far-fetched that Freddie could have been confused as well.

"It was a young lady," Ryan replied. "So I don't think it was Freddie unless that's short for something else."

"Freddie's a male," Mariah mumbled, staring down at the bag. Her name was clearly written on the slip but the apartment number was smeared. That explained the misguided delivery. "She must be new. I hope Freddie is okay and not sick or anything."

"Is Freddie a friend of yours?"

"Kind of."

How did one go about explaining the significance of regular food delivery? Especially to an ex-boyfriend.

Ryan's gaze darted over Mariah's shoulder and into the empty apartment. "Are you having a party?"

"A party?"

Wow, I'm so eloquent tonight. I sound like a genius.

She simply hadn't expected to see him this quickly. She'd needed more time to…prepare. Build up some defenses.

"The bag was pretty heavy."

"Oh. That. Well…I order food for a few days so I don't have to worry about it."

"You used to do that when we were in college. You'd order extra pizza so we could have some the next day."

She had done that although she hadn't given it a thought in years. And he'd remembered it.

"It's a bad habit. I could just order again tomorrow." She looked back down at the bag and then up at him. "Have you eaten yet?"

Now why did I say that? Am I stupid? Yes. Yes, I am. I'm an idiot.

"No." He glanced back at his open door. "I was going to cook something."

"You can cook?"

The words tumbled out before she could stop them. She didn't mean to sound shocked but...she *was* shocked. Ryan hadn't known how to boil water when they were together, but then he'd never had to cook for himself.

Laughing, he nodded. "I've learned to cook. People can change, you know."

They could but Ryan had always been so stubborn about changing anything about himself. He took great pride in acting like a jackass. It was a Beck family trait.

"If you say so."

He sniffed appreciatively at the air which was filled with the most delicious aroma of tomatoes and garlic.

"I really should cook my own dinner tonight. Liza brought over a ton of groceries for me."

"She told me she'd done that."

"You talked to her today?"

"Yes. She said you were going to see the Harringtons."

"I did visit them."

They seemed to have run out of conversation. Funny, how when they were together they could talk for hours and hours. They'd never seemed to get bored of one another. Now? They were staring at each other awkwardly in her doorway.

Ryan glanced quickly over his shoulder. "I guess I should let you eat your dinner. I need to figure something out for my own too."

Shit.

Mariah had been brought up to be polite even when she didn't want to be. It wasn't that she didn't want to be nice to Ryan – she did – it just wasn't easy to be around him. But that was her problem, not his.

In fact, inviting him in to share her dinner would probably be a good thing. She'd get used to seeing him again, being around him and then it wouldn't be such a big deal. Clearly, avoiding each other hadn't worked. This just might be a good plan. She'd see that he was still an asshole and that would help ease the ache that seemed to have taken up residence in her chest the moment she'd opened the door.

Dammit, I'm thinking about the past far too much.

"Why don't you just join me for dinner? I have plenty of food."

"I couldn't do that."

His denial was swift and sure although his body might not be in complete agreement. He'd leaned in a little bit and sniffed the air again.

"Sure you can. It's just food."

"I shouldn't."

This was the Ryan she knew well. Full of contradictions.

"You say no but did you realize that you nodded your head? Your stomach has other ideas."

That stomach took the opportunity to let its needs be known by making a hungry, gurgling sound that they both could hear. Ryan's hand went directly to his belly as if to cover up the noise but it was too late.

"Just get in here," Mariah said in a brisk, no nonsense tone. What she needed right now was a huge dose of practicality. That was usually Ryan's job, and she'd been the dreaming artist. Maybe they both had changed. "Sitting in the same room eating food won't kill us. We did it for your sister's wedding."

"I don't think it's a good idea."

Yet, he hadn't taken a step back. He'd actually taken a step *forward*. He was officially out of her doorway and into her apartment.

"We can go back to avoiding each other in about an hour. In the meantime, I'll unpack the food and you can play hard to get."

Although he probably wasn't playing. She, on the other hand...

Nope, she wasn't going all gooey-eyed at her ex. She'd learned hard lessons since their breakup. Lesson number one? Men don't change unless they want to. And they rarely want to.

"I'm not avoiding you."

"Bull hockey," she shot back, sliding the bag onto the kitchen counter. "As my beloved father would say. We were both trying to avoid each other at the reception. We did a decent job of it too, but I wouldn't say that it's helped much. It's still weird and awkward."

Times ten.

Ryan's brows shot up. "I am not awkward. Or weird."

"I said the situation is awkward and weird, not that you were. Now, go close your door and come and eat. I'm not taking no for an answer. Avoiding each other got us nowhere so now we're going to try something different."

"How different?"

"Maybe we can be friends."

It sounded ludicrous even to her own ears. Or did it? She and Ryan had always been friends even before they were a couple. She'd certainly missed him these last years. He'd never been boring that was for sure.

"You want to be friends with me?"

"I think it's better than ducking into bathrooms whenever we see one another. We have to get through your mother's party and Brad's memorial service. So far, we haven't done a great job. We were always friends and good ones, too."

"I don't really need any more friends."

Now this was the Ryan Beck she'd known and loved. Stubborn as a mule. She'd learned not to take any of his crap and give as could as he gave. A woman had to be strong to deal with a man like that. She'd learned about boundaries and sticking to them.

"Whatever. I'm going to eat. You can stand there like an idiot or you can join me. I'm not going to waste my breath."

Turning her back on him, she began to gather plates, napkins, and forks, not daring to look back and see what he was doing. If he wanted to huff back to his apartment, he was welcome to but she was going to make sure he looked petty doing it. She left his plate of food on the counter and took her own back into the living room, turning on the television and then curling up on the corner of the couch. She could see that he was just standing there but she ignored him, taking a bite of the delicious food and thinking that he should eat while it was hot.

The wafting aroma of mouthwatering food must have eventually got to him because he finally picked up his own plate and sat down on the couch as well.

With a cushion between them.

Your virtue is safe with me, asshole.

Ryan might be gorgeous but she wasn't so hard up for male companionship that she'd jump his bones without warning or at least an invitation.

They didn't speak until their plates were empty and their stomachs full. Mariah took the dishes into the kitchen and rinsed them off before loading them into the dishwasher.

"Glass of wine? I was thinking that I'd have one."

She didn't wait for him to respond, simply pulling down two glasses. If he didn't want any, he'd stop her before she poured the wine.

"Let me do that," he said, taking the corkscrew from her hand. Their fingers had brushed and she felt the old familiar heat she remembered from his touch.

Now that's inconvenient. Crap. I was afraid that would happen.

"I can do it myself," she said but she didn't try to get the corkscrew back or protest any more. "I don't need a man to open a bottle of wine."

"I was trying to be helpful."

Right, and she was the Queen of England.

"You were trying to show me that I didn't know what I was doing and that you were better at it. Being the best is important to you."

It wasn't his fault though. It had been drilled into him by Jack and Patricia Beck. His parents had much to answer for. Poor Ryan had never had a chance.

"That's not true."

Mariah had to hide her laughter at his denial.

"Whatever you say."

Clearly, she'd annoyed him.

"No, it's not whatever I say. You said it. Own it."

Did he think she wouldn't?

"Fine, I said it and I own it. You like to be the best, Ryan. This cannot be news to you at this point in your life. It was a huge bone of contention between us when we were dating."

He finished pouring the wine and pushed a glass toward her. "I don't remember any of this. Maybe you're thinking of another guy."

"I don't think I could confuse you with anyone else. Are you denying that you're competitive as hell? Because I have vivid memories of you getting pissy because you lost a Monopoly game to me one New Year's Eve. Or how about the time that I did better on a Chemistry exam than you did? You acted like a jackwagon then too. Basically, any time anyone else does something better than you, you get butthurt."

"That's not true."

Mariah took a sip of the rich cabernet before responding. She shouldn't have opened this can of worms but now that she had...

"So you're denying that any of that ever happened?"

"I'm denying that it bothered me," he said, his tone defensive. "I did not get *butthurt*. Hell, I was happy for you. I was always your biggest cheerleader, Mariah."

"Really? Are you sure? Because you spent most of that day trying to figure out how I scored so well on that exam. You did everything but accuse me of cheating."

"I did not think you cheated," he protested loudly. "I never thought that."

"But you couldn't believe that I'd scored that high," she shot back. "It was like you'd come upon the mystery of the universe and simply couldn't comprehend how I'd managed it."

He'd lifted the glass to his lips but before taking a drink he slammed it back down on the counter.

"Now, come on. Give me a break. Admit that you were more surprised than I was. You were flunking Chemistry up until that point. Your grades were abysmal by your own admission. So I think you should cut me so damn slack when I'm surprised that you pull an A on the midterm."

She had been flunking chemistry. She'd thought she was

going to go down the traditional route of getting her degree and then getting a job, maybe even joining her parents' health food business but in the end, she'd wanted to do her art more. After completing her freshman year, she'd transferred to an art school. Ryan hadn't been happy about that but she'd been determined.

"Yes, I was doing badly," she agreed. "But I'd hired that tutor and buckled down to study hard. How could you be so shocked when I'd received good grades in high school? I was capable, I just hated science classes."

And math. She'd liked psychology and philosophy and tolerated English.

"Excuse me for being surprised that you raised your grade from a D to an A."

"You still can't do it, can you?" she laughed. "Even now, all these years later you hate to admit that you were wrong. Well...you were. Get over it."

"I can admit when I'm wrong."

"You can but you don't like to. You'll go down every other path until it's the only option available to you. You're so much like your father."

The words were out before she could stop them. It was absolutely the wrong thing to say even if it was true. It was a sure-fire way to piss off Ryan, and she wasn't even trying to do that.

"I am not like my father," he said through gritted teeth. A muscled jumped in his jaw and his cheeks had turned slightly red. He was angry. "I wasn't then and I'm not now."

"I don't want to argue with you, Ryan."

"You want us to be friends."

He said it like it was completely out of the question. Perhaps he was right. He was too much work at the moment.

"I was hoping we could. We have a few things in common. Like how much we both love Liza. It would be far easier for her if we could get along."

"I can get along if you wouldn't always bring up the past."

He didn't want to talk about the past? Fine. She could deal with that.

"Okay, let's talk about the present. Tell me about your new job and how you're going to find out who killed Brad."

Because even Ryan Beck was going to have his hands full with trying to solve a murder from over a decade ago.

CHAPTER SEVEN

RYAN HAD CONVENIENTLY forgotten how challenging being around Mariah could be. She didn't take any of his crap and never had. On more than one occasion, his own mother had advised him to seek out an easier to be with girlfriend.

Funny, they hadn't argued that much but he'd often be frustrated by her stubborn nature. She'd accused him of being bull-headed but she was no innocent angel either. He used to swear that if he said the sky was blue she'd argue that it was actually a shade of green. She was contrary like that although she would have just told him that he wasn't right all the time.

He'd never thought that he was. Right?

I didn't. I'm sure of it.

Toward the end of their relationship, their disagreements had become more frequent until they'd mutually ended it. Their lives were heading into completely different directions – him a cop and her an artist. It hadn't been an easy decision but in the long run he was positive it had been the right thing to do. They couldn't have made it work in the long term no matter how much in love they were. Wasn't that what everyone always said?

Love alone isn't enough. A couple had to have more.

But this was Mariah. The one person he'd never bullshitted in his life about anything. She'd asked him a straight question. He didn't have a good reason for not answering honestly.

"I don't know," he finally confessed after taking a sip of the wine. He wasn't a big red wine drinker but this wasn't bad. "I don't know how I'm going to find out what happened to Brad. We don't even know that anyone killed him yet, remember? It could have been an accident."

He was hoping that was the case.

"Do you think it was an accident?"

"I don't know enough about the case to give an answer," he said honestly. "I'll know more when I see the case file and evidence tomorrow. I might have an opinion then."

Mariah's gaze was on her wine glass, studying the contents. "I keep thinking back to that night. I can't get it out of my mind since we heard they found Brad."

"Me too."

Her head jerked up, her green eyes bright with tears. Even weepy, she was an extraordinarily beautiful woman with her long dark hair and curvy figure. She wasn't fashion model tall but somehow she managed to have legs that went on for days. Right now, they were bared and golden by a tattered pair of running shorts.

"What do you remember about that night? Sometimes I think that my memories are all messed up and that I'm not thinking about it straight. What do you remember?"

Images from that night crowded his brain. He'd spent so much time thinking about that night after it happened and then he'd pushed it away for a long time. It had all come roaring back though since his meeting with Logan. He couldn't get away from the past.

Hell, his past was standing across from him right now.

"I remember that it was raining," he began, letting the memories take him back. "There was a thunderstorm and you don't like lightning and thunder."

"Lots of people don't like storms."

Mariah didn't have to be defensive. She had a terrible fear of storms after getting caught in one while walking her dog when she was about eight. Her parents had driven the neighborhood looking for her and found her wet and crying, huddled under a tree and hugging her dog. She always tried to act like storms didn't bother her, but he knew that they did.

"That's true. Many people don't like them."

"I just didn't want to get my new shoes wet."

They'd briefly disagreed about going out. Mariah hadn't wanted to at first but he'd talked her into it, reminding her that they wouldn't stay late. They had a plane to catch in the morning.

"But I convinced you to go."

"Yes, and we did have a good time."

They had but back then it had been easy to have fun. They'd been young and their friends, music, and a few drinks were all it took to entertain them.

"We got there after everyone else," Ryan went on. "Brad was already there along with the rest of our friends."

By the time they'd arrived, the rain had luckily stopped but the bad weather had kept the crowd down in the bar. Normally, it was packed shoulder to shoulder.

"Trent and Caroline were on the dance floor," Mariah said. "Because Brad didn't like to dance."

Caroline and Brad had been an item of sorts, dating on and off for years, although the latter had been a rotten boyfriend.

"Brad just didn't think he looked cool when he danced," Ryan said. "And for good reason. He was a lousy dancer. Brad and Dan were doing shots, I think."

"Sex on the beach shots," Mariah agreed. "Because we were all going to Hawaii the next day. Dan ordered us shots too. Carl and Theo, however, weren't doing shots. They were playing pool in the corner. Mike was watching and he was going to play the winner."

Carl didn't like to drink much because alcoholism ran in his family. His dad might be the president of a huge bank but he was also a drunk. A mean one. Carl had spent as much time as possible away from home.

Mike had always been a cautious person and that night was no exception. From what Ryan could remember, his friend – and now brother in law – had nursed a couple of beers all night. From what Mike had said on the plane the next day, he'd left soon after Ryan and Mariah.

Theo was like Mike in that respect. He didn't binge drink

like so many young people, keeping to a few beers all night and maybe doing a shot or two. On his birthday, he'd thrown caution to the wind and ended up drunker than a skunk and puked most of the next morning. Since then, he'd been wary as hell.

Dan and Brad? They were the original party animals. They'd start pre-gaming at home before they even headed out to a bar. They loved rowdy crowds, loud music, easy women, and lots of booze. As far as they were concerned, life was one never ending party and last call just meant they had to move to a new location.

"We had a table in the corner," Ryan said. "Dan and Brad were knocking back shots as fast as the waitress could bring them. At one point, Caroline came over and tried to get Brad to leave but he wouldn't go."

"She knew she was wasting her time," Mariah replied. "Brad never did anything he didn't want to do."

"I'd say we were all like that."

More than a little spoiled.

"He had it down to an art form though, and you would know. You went to boarding school with him. Didn't you say he was constantly in trouble?"

Ryan didn't have to tell anyone because Brad would brag about it. He'd loved playing pranks and breaking rules. In fact, he went out of his way to break rules.

Even the Bro Code Rules.

"He's lucky he didn't get punched in the mouth more often."

"You're thinking about that night. It wasn't a big deal. I handled it."

"You shouldn't have had to handle it at all. He should have known better."

They both knew what night Ryan was thinking about. It had been Spring Break and their families had rented houses in the Caribbean – all in a row. The adults had shuttled the teenagers off into one house so they could make noise and wouldn't bother the grownups. To this day, Ryan couldn't believe his parents and the others had done that. He sure as hell wouldn't be doing anything like that with his kids. It was asking for trouble.

Brad, as usual, was being a jerk to Caroline, flirting outrageously with other girls and generally being a dick. She'd finally had enough, slapped his face, and stomped out, taking several of her friends with her. Eventually Brad had camped out in the kitchen feeling sorry for himself. When Mariah had come in there to get a fresh soda, he'd tried to get some sympathy, and with her being soft-hearted she'd tried to comfort him.

In a friendly way.

She'd given him an inch and he'd tried to take a mile, getting handsy with her until she'd had to knee him in the balls. Brad had yelled, causing everyone to run into the kitchen to see what was going on. Mariah looked pissed. Brad was yelling and saying that she'd lost her mind. She'd told Ryan what had happened and then she told Brad that she wasn't sorry. He needed to learn to keep his hands to himself.

And he had. Brad had never tried anything with Mariah

again, although he'd pulled that crap with most of the other females in their group more than once.

As for Ryan, his close friendship with Brad had never been the same. At one point, they'd been more like brothers, but after Brad's actions with Mariah, Ryan had put some distance between them. He simply couldn't trust him the same way.

I should have punched him that night. He'd deserved it.

"But I did handle it," Mariah said, breaking into his thoughts. "He was always that way, pushing at every boundary he came across. Sometimes, I wonder if that's what happened to him. Did he run into the wrong person that night? Did someone take offense to something that he did?"

She spoke the last part so softly Ryan almost didn't hear the words.

"I've often wondered about that myself," he confessed. "Brad could be so naive about the world at times. He thought everyone was just like him. Just out for a good time."

"Everything was a game," she whispered into her glass, taking another sip. "It was all fun."

"Until he disappeared."

She set the glass down and pushed it away slightly. "When was the last time you saw him? What did he say?"

"He was at the pool table with Theo and Carl. Caroline and Daphne were there, too. I told him that you and I were going to leave. He said that he was going to stay and have some more fun. He wanted to win back some money from Carl at pool after he took a leak. He headed to the bathroom and that's the last time I saw him."

Mariah nodded. "I saw him in the hallway. I was coming out the ladies' room so we could leave and he was going into the men's room. He didn't see me, I don't think, but that's the last time I saw him. Do you think that he walked out of the back door? Cameras never saw him walk out the front."

Ryan had already thought about that. "It was an emergency door and had an alarm on it. We've both heard it go off and there's no way someone wouldn't have heard it. It was loud as hell. I don't see how he could have walked out of it without everyone knowing."

"Then how could he get outside and into the construction site next door?"

"That's what I need to find out."

"Can you? Really? After all these years?"

"I'm going to do my best. It's what Brad and his family de-serves." Ryan paused but his mouth didn't. "I'm not that thrilled to be here, if I'm honest. I just want to do my job and get back to my life."

Now why did I say that out loud?

Her expression changed from sad to angry in an instant.

"I feel sorry for your parents and Liza. They love you, you know, but you act like they're the worst people on earth."

"I don't," he replied reflexively. "I love Liza. I adore her. But you know I have a difficult relationship with Jack and Pat."

Crossing her arms over her chest, she shook her head. "I noticed that you didn't say that you loved them. They're your parents, Ryan. They raised you and gave you everything."

"Yes, everything that money could buy."

She rolled her eyes and groaned. "You're upset because you didn't have the parents of your dreams. But your parents were fine. Give me a break."

She didn't get it and she never had.

"You wouldn't understand. Your parents are all touchy-feely hippies that said I love you every day of your life. I bet you got a hug and praise when you graduated high school. In fact, I know you did. My dad told me that I needed to buckle down for college."

"Your mom and dad bought you a BMW for high school graduation. I think that's praise. I'm sorry that you didn't get a hug as well. I know what that would have meant for you but Jack and Pat just aren't huggers. It doesn't make them bad parents, it just makes them emotionally closed off. But if you think they don't love you, you're delusional. They love you. They just don't know how to say it. So they show it. With stuff."

"Maybe I didn't want *stuff*."

Sighing, Mariah reached across the counter and placed her hand on his. The skin burned where she touched it as if it was 2008 again.

You can't go back in time.

"You're one of the smartest people I've ever known, but the one thing you don't get is that people aren't always what you want them to be, Ryan. Your life would be a lot easier if you stopped expecting people to change for you, and then being upset when they don't or can't. The fact is some people can easily say I love you without actually feeling it. Your parents can feel it but they can't say it. I know which one I'd rather have but you have to make your own decisions." She leaned forward so they were nose to nose. "By the way, you're not exactly Mr. Eloquent. You rarely told me you loved me when we were together. You rarely let me in any of your emotions, for that matter, so basically you're the pot in this scenario and your parents are the kettle."

He could feel the heat of anger on the back of his neck. She was twisting the past into something that it wasn't.

"I think you and I don't remember the past the same."

She shrugged. "Maybe we don't."

He stepped back, trying to get some breathing room. It was always like this with Mariah.

She was intense and she challenged him at every turn. He didn't want tonight to turn into a battle. Or a war.

"This is why I'm not sure we can be friends."

Brushing by him, she marched over to the door and opened it. For a split second, he'd felt the heat of her body and smelled her distinct perfume. It was sultry and spicy and at one point in his life it had made him crazy with lust.

But no more. I'm immune.

Fuck that, who am I kidding? One hour in her company and I'm like a teenage kid again.

"Then you should probably go," she said, still holding the door open. "I'll try and avoid you as much as possible. Good luck with the investigation."

He hesitated for a moment but her expression was clear – he was an asshole. She was done with him…at least for now. This was why he'd ended their relationship. They didn't see things the same way.

"Thank you for dinner," he said, moving toward the door. "I really don't want us to be at each other's throats. I just–"

"Don't want to be friends," she said, finishing his sentence before he could. "Got it. I think you're right. You haven't changed a bit, Ryan, and that's not a good thing. So good night."

He didn't argue. There was no point. Instead he exited her apartment and entered his own, shutting the door behind him. Blowing out a long breath, he leaned back against the door.

The woman made him insane. He couldn't think straight when they were breathing the same air, so close together. His mind got all muddled up and the next thing he knew he was saying shit he never would have if he'd had his head on straight. He hadn't meant to hurt her and he realized that he had. She'd taken his statement about being friends personally when it wasn't about her. It was about him.

He doubted she was going to believe him about that though. Best thing he could do is make sure that they weren't alone again. There was too much…*history* between them.

History and heat. At least on his side.

He might be digging into the past because of Brad's death but that didn't mean that having any sort of relationship with Mariah was a good idea.

Do a job. Go home. That was the plan.

CHAPTER EIGHT

"**Y**OUR BROTHER IS an idiot. A total and complete dumbass."

Mariah was sitting in an outdoor cafe having breakfast with Liza the next day. She'd been simmering all last night and this morning about Ryan's stubborn behavior.

"Good morning to you too," Liza joked, pouring cream into her coffee. "I guess you and Ryan have seen each other then."

"My food was accidentally delivered to him last night," Mariah grumbled, perusing the menu. They had great omelets here. "So I invited him in for dinner. I thought we might be able to be friends. Now I'm wondering what I ever saw in him. He lives in a deep state of denial. He thinks he's not stubborn or super competitive. Can you believe that?"

Liza burst into laughter, her cheeks turning pink. "Of course I can, he's a Beck. For the most part, we're deeply in denial about how our upbringing has affected our psyche. Ryan thinks he's so smart but he's just like the rest of us in so many ways. I can actually hear him telling you that he's not competitive in the least and that winning doesn't matter to him. He believes it, too.

At least I can admit it. I hate to lose. More than I like to win. It's a family trait and it was bred into us from the day we were born."

"He thinks his parents don't love him," Mariah went on. "Then he said that I couldn't understand how he felt because my parents were different."

"In a way, he has a point. You can *sympathize* but you can't *empathize*. But it's crazy that he thinks Mom and Dad don't love him."

"I know, right? Your parents adore him and he can't see it."

"He can't see that he's just like Dad either."

"I think he does see it, but he's in denial about that, too. I think he's convinced himself that if he left the family and made his own way that somehow he'd magically become different."

They had to pause the conversation as the server took their order. A Denver omelet for Mariah with a side of wheat toast and orange juice, and a Belgian waffle for Liza.

"I'm off my diet today," she declared after handing her menu to the waitress. "I'm going to be bad."

Calories didn't dare come near Liza. Like her brother she was tall, slim, and gorgeous.

Mariah was lucky as well, her metabolism lightning fast. Someday it might turn on her but right now she could eat whatever she wanted. Unfortunately, what she wanted most of the time wasn't good for her.

That's how it is with Ryan, too. He's not good for me.

But damn, he looked handsome last night.

Ryan Beck was like a giant hot fudge sundae. Decadent and delicious but she'd probably have a tummy ache afterward and lots of regret.

"So you invited my brother in for dinner and then told him off? I'm guessing he didn't take it well."

Mariah shrugged as if it didn't matter in the least. Because it didn't.

"I told him that he should leave so I have no idea if he was pissed off or butthurt. I told him that he hadn't changed and that wasn't a good thing. I also told him that it was clear that we don't see the past the same way."

"Ryan has changed," Liza replied with another laugh. "But he's still stubborn. And a little introspection wouldn't hurt him either. That's something that the Beck family lacks. As a rule we don't delve too deeply into our motivations."

"Ryan thinks that money is the only Beck motivation."

"He'd be wrong. We like power, too," Liza said with a giggle. "Sounds like you two had quite the blowout last night."

"Actually, it wasn't until the end. We talked about that last night with Brad and what we both remembered. It was okay. Then it just…took a bad turn. I didn't want to argue with him. I was hoping we could be friends. You know, for you."

"For me?"

"I thought it would be easier on you if Ryan and I could get along."

Liza nodded in understanding. "I see. For me."

"Right. For you."

Liza's lips were twitching with laughter. Again.

"Did I say something funny?"

"Yes, and this time it's you being completely unaware. I'm not sure you're doing all of this for me, hon. Maybe you're doing it for you."

"Me? How so?"

Liza glanced around the restaurant and then leaned forward. "Can you honestly say that you never think about Ryan and what might have been?"

"What kind of question is that? I don't dwell in the past. I've moved on. It's been years. We're complete different people now."

"You just said that Ryan hadn't changed."

Sighing, Mariah tried to explain herself. "I meant that he hadn't changed about a few things, not that he hadn't changed at all. I barely even know the person he's become."

"He's basically the same person but more mature. He's a good man."

"I didn't say he wasn't."

"You said he was an idiot."

"A good man can be a little dimwitted."

Liza signaled the waitress for more coffee. "When are you going to admit that you're not over Ryan? There's a part of you that still cares about him."

"No, I don't," Mariah denied immediately. "I mean…of course I care about him as a person. I wouldn't want to see him hurt or sick, but I don't *care*-care about him."

Liza raised one perfectly shaped eyebrow. "Then why do you care if he's an idiot or not?"

Opening her mouth, the words stuck in Mariah's throat. She didn't have an answer. Not a good one, anyway.

"Because he's your brother. And he thinks he's so smart."

"Okay, I believe you."

Do I believe myself? Seeing Ryan has turned me inside out.

THE NEXT MORNING Ryan met Detective Peter Rosenthal, the officer that had been assigned to the case. To be honest, he wasn't sure what he was walking into. Some police officers welcomed consultants and private investigators and some didn't. Whether Rosenthal would be the cooperating type remained to be seen.

After arriving at the station, Ryan was led into a bullpen-type of office setup, which wasn't unusual. Lots of desks pushed together in a small space so there wasn't much privacy but Ryan wasn't shown to any of those desks. He was led even deeper into the office to a small conference room in a back corner. A man a few years older than himself was sitting at the small table paging through a folder and drinking a cup of coffee. There was a cardboard box on the table next to him.

"Detective Rosenthal?"

The person who had escorted Ryan had disappeared and this was the destination, so…

"That's me. You must be Ryan Beck."

The man stood and shook Ryan's hand. He was a few inches shorter with a stocky build and graying hair. Hopefully that meant experience. They could use that on this case.

"I am."

Rosenthal chuckled a little and waved toward the second chair. "Jesus, you're young. Or am I just old? I swear the new recruits are starting to look like kids to me. Maybe I should start thinking about retirement."

"I'd be bored to death in retirement."

Ryan could barely sit still for more than thirty minutes at a time. He didn't sleep much either. Last night, after his argument with Mariah, he'd managed a whopping four hours. Luckily, he was used to it.

"Damn straight. Me too, actually. I'll probably die on the job. Now, can I get you a cup of coffee? It's terrible but it's hot."

"I'm good, but thanks." Ryan sat down, the legs of the chair scraping on the gray tile. "I was hoping we could talk about Brad Harrington's case. Is the coroner report in yet?"

Rosenthal tapped the papers in front of him. "I got it this morning. It looks like blunt force trauma to the head. There's a dent in the side of his skull that matches the shape of the metal pipe found near the body."

"So…murder?"

It left a nasty taste in Ryan's mouth to even say it. This was what he hadn't wanted to hear.

"It looks that way. I doubt he accidentally fell and hit the side of his head on a pipe."

"I made you copies of the official case file," Rosenthal went on. "It includes all the statements from the time of the disappearance plus the photos from the site where the body was found. The little evidence we were able to find is in this box but I'm afraid I can't let you take it. I can let you look at it, though, and you're welcome to take pictures."

"That's very accommodating of you. I appreciate that."

"I'm guessing you don't always get a warm welcome when you show up," the other man said with a grimace. "Personally, I'm glad that you're here to take the lead on this case. Skip Harrington has been breathing down the necks of the mayor, the governor, both senators, and God knows who else. They in turn scream at my boss who screams at me. I don't like to be yelled at. I'm funny that way. So you being here is going to take the heat off of me. I'll let you deal with the powers that be, and I'll just do my job."

"I don't have a problem dealing with Skip Harrington."

"Better you than me. My boss said that you were friends with the victim. I'm sorry for your loss. I should have said that first thing, and for that I apologize."

"Thank you. It was a long time ago. We were childhood friends. Brad was basically a good guy. He sure as hell didn't deserve this, no matter what happened that night."

Rosenthal was giving him that look...one that was questioning whether Ryan was wealthy as well, but then also wondering why he would be a former cop.

Ryan wouldn't be giving the officer the details of his relationship with the Harringtons.

"So what are your next steps and how can I assist you?" Rosenthal asked. "We're stretched thin as hell here but this case is high profile and we're under pressure to close it as quickly as possible."

"After I look through this file and evidence, I'm going to visit the site and take a look around. I'll also re-interview everyone that I can find from that night."

The detective was nodding as he took another sip of coffee. "We've definitely got our work cut out for us here."

"There is something that you can do to help me, actually."

"Name it."

"The Harringtons mentioned a serial killer that was working Chicago at that time killing college kids. I don't remember seeing anything in the papers about it but I'd like to take a look at the case files to see if there are any similarities."

"That was never proven." Rosenthal scowled and placed his cup down on the table. "It was only one detective's theory that got picked up by the newspapers. There was no serial killer offing college kids."

"I'd like to look at the files anyway," Ryan replied in his most soothing tone. He wanted to keep the cops on his side and cooperating. "That way I can tell the parents that I did my due diligence. I had some information that my firm pulled for me but I want to make sure that I cover all of my bases."

"If that's what you want. I'll get the files pulled and have them messengered to you. Where should I have them sent?"

Ryan pulled out his little notebook and scribbled down his address, making sure that his apartment number was legible. He didn't want any morbid crime scene photos being delivered to Mariah by accident like last night's dinner.

They talked for a few more minutes, splitting the work with Ryan taking on the lion's share. That's what he was there for, after all; plus he was familiar with most of the people involved.

The detective left Ryan alone to look through the evidence of which there was not much. Brad's clothes, his phone and wallet. That was it.

The phone was a complete write-off after years of rain and snow. The screen was cracked as well and Ryan couldn't help wonder how that had happened. It hadn't been cracked earlier that fateful evening. He was sure of that.

Each piece that was inside the wallet had been taken out and preserved in a plastic bag. There was the usual – driver's license, credit cards, a condom, and a few faded photos, weathered from the elements, but surprisingly clear. The heavy leather of the wallet must have protected them.

Ryan copied down the credit card numbers so that he could run them to see Brad's spending habits.

But the pictures…

One was of Brad and his brother Sebastien, both smiling and happy as if they didn't have a care in the world. From the background, it looked like the day that Brad had started college and they were helping him move into the dorms.

The second photo was of Caroline, a candid shot when they

were out partying one night.

The third photo was all of the guys – including Ryan – taken in Aspen. He had a clear memory of that day. They'd spent hours skiing and having fun, and they'd eventually hit the ski lodge for a hot drink, purely non-alcoholic because none of them were of age. Carl had asked a man at the next table to take their picture.

I have the same one in a scrapbook at home.

An actual photograph on paper. Not a digital image on his phone. Carl had made sure that everyone had a copy as a souvenir. As if Ryan would ever forget that trip. Had it been the best vacation ever? Maybe. It sure seemed like it at the time. They'd all been around eighteen and looking forward to graduating high school and going on to college. Their parents were friends and decided to take this trip and for once they'd given Ryan and his pals a hell of a lot more freedom than they ever had before.

The only thing they were expected to do was meet their parents for dinner in the evening. That was it. The rest of the time they could do as they pleased. All of them had had the time of their lives just hanging out with one another and goofing around. It felt like the world belonged to them and that anything was possible. At times, Ryan missed that feeling of invincibility that only someone young can truly feel. He'd been so sure about everything back then, certain that he knew it all.

Now? He didn't know shit. Was that the definition of maturity? When you realize that you don't know anything?

He took pictures of the bagged evidence with his phone and then packed it back into the box. His stomach was queasy from the coffee he'd drank this morning. Seeing a young man's life summed up in one cardboard box didn't sit well with him. No one deserved to have their life cut short like that, though. No one. It made him more determined than ever to find out what happened that night. Brad deserved it and so did his family.

On his way out of the station, Ryan thanked the detective for his help and they set a time the next day to touch base again. He needed to put some food into his stomach but instead found himself heading straight for the lot where they'd found Brad's body. Food could wait for a little while longer. He needed to see the scene after all of these years. Paying the cab driver, Ryan stepped out onto the sidewalk in front of the construction site.

But apparently, he wasn't the only one with the same thought. He had company on that sidewalk.

Mariah.

What was she doing here?

CHAPTER NINE

MARIAH SHOULD HAVE known that Ryan would show up here. He might have even told her he was coming here when he was at her apartment last night. Was he the one that had put this in her head?

She didn't need to turn around to see him. She could feel him next to her.

"I keep thinking that there had to be something we could have done that night," she said out loud, surprising herself. Last night she'd made a promise to avoid him and now she was confessing her deepest thoughts. "Something that would have changed this."

"I've wondered that myself but damned if I can come up with anything."

"We could have stayed with him. Maybe…we shouldn't have left that night."

"We left him many nights still partying. He wanted to stay up all night and he was an adult. He didn't want us babysitting him."

She knew that too, but…

"Intellectually, I know that. But emotionally, it's another story."

"I know what you're saying. I still keeping thinking about that night, wondering if I've missed anything or anyone but I come up with nothing new."

There was silence as they both stood there looking at the construction site. Yellow crime scene tape was wrapped around the place where they'd found Brad.

"I haven't been back here in years," she finally said. "Not since you and I came here. I don't even know why I'm here now."

They'd come together not long after Brad's disappearance, but they hadn't really known what they were looking for. They hadn't known he was only twenty feet away under a layer of earth and concrete.

"Because it's new again," he said. "You're here because we're all reminded of Brad."

This time she turned to look at him. He looked handsome as always today, dressed casually in khaki pants and a button-down shirt, the sleeves rolled up as a concession to the summer heat in Chicago.

"Is that why you're here?"

He shook his head. "I'm here to look at the site where they found him. Take some pictures."

"So this is work?"

"Yes, although I'll admit that I was planning to get a bite to eat but ended up here instead. I guess that's where my mind was at so I'm just going to go with it."

Ryan began to walk toward the crime scene area, but Mariah hesitated. She wasn't sure she was even allowed to go near it. She didn't want to go past the yellow tape. There wouldn't be a bloody scene or anything but it was hard to think of anything but Brad and the past already. If she saw the place where his body was found, she might never sleep at all.

She stayed where she was as he began snapping a few photos with his phone. Then he walked over to the back door of the bar, eyeing it up and down. This time she followed him.

"You said yourself that the door had an alarm on it."

"I'm not looking at the door." He pointed to a small window about two feet from the exit. "I'm looking at that window."

There was a matching one on the opposite side of the door. One was in the men's' restroom and one was in the women's. They were both about six or seven feet off the ground but a grown man wouldn't have any trouble with the distance. But he might with the width and length of the window itself. It wasn't big. She could easily fit through it, but a man?

"I'm not sure that Brad could fit through there," she said, her gaze following his. "He wasn't a big guy but that window is pretty small."

"He was about five-nine and didn't weigh above a buck-fifty. He could fit. That's the type of window that lifts all the way up."

"Okay, I'll play. Let's say that Brad did crawl out of a window that night. Why? Why on earth would he do that? It doesn't make any sense."

Stroking his chin, Ryan didn't take his gaze from the window. "Maybe because someone was waiting for him outside the front door. We don't know everything that he was into."

"You said it yourself, though. It could have been an accident."

Ryan shook his head. "Blunt force trauma to the head. Medical examiner thinks it could have been a pipe from this construction site."

"And you think it's homicide? He could have fallen out of the window and hit his head."

She didn't want to think that someone had killed Brad, although that thought had occurred to her before. Many times. She'd always hoped she was wrong.

"That is a possibility but remember that the indentation in his skull had a specific shape. Unless he fell on a cylindrical object, of course. My gut is telling me that someone hit him in the side of the head."

Shuddering, Mariah's gaze went back to the window. "So you think that Brad climbed out to get away from someone but it didn't work and they hit him in the head with a pipe?"

"It's way too early to be making any sort of theories. At this point, I'm simply gathering possibilities. That's all."

"But your gut has drawn a conclusion?"

He turned to her, his brows raised in question. "Sounds like you don't believe in gut-hunches? My boss caught a serial killer following his gut."

"Wade Bryson." She'd heard the stories as much as everyone

else had, the newspaper articles and the news reports on television. It had been big news for weeks. At least until a bigger story came along and knocked it out of the headlines. "And I do believe in listening to my gut. When it talks."

"It will talk more if you listen to it."

"I'll be more attentive. What else is your gut telling you?"

"That I need to eat. I'm starving and I can't concentrate when I'm this hungry. I want to talk to the manager of the bar but they won't be here this early in the morning. I'll have to come back later."

"A good meal can always make the brain work a little better."

He slipped his sunglasses back on. "Then let's go. There's a cafe just down the block."

She knew that, of course. They'd been there before. Together.

"Are you inviting me to eat with you?"

"Yes. I'm planning on apologizing too. So you won't want to miss that."

Considering she'd never heard him apologize to her, she definitely didn't want to miss that. This was an event of monumental proportions. Maybe he had changed, just a little.

"Lead the way."

To her surprise he took her hand, a frisson of electricity running up her arm and straight to her heart. She was so distracted by her inconvenient reaction that she didn't hear or see the speeding car heading straight for them as they were in the crosswalk. It was only when Ryan dragged her to the safety of the sidewalk that she realized what had happened.

"Holy hell, he needs to slow down," she gasped, picking up her purse where it had fallen to the pavement. Ryan was scowling at the road and the car had disappeared. "Thanks for thinking fast."

"That idiot could have killed us both," he ground out, muttering a not so nice word under his breath. "Where could he be going in such a damn hurry?"

"Maybe he had an emergency."

"You always try to think the best of people," Ryan laughed. "I think he was probably just a jerk driving like an asshole."

"Or he might just be a jackass," Mariah agreed. "We'll never know. He's gone anyway, and hopefully he won't run down any more innocent pedestrians."

Ryan gave one last disgusted look in the direction that the car had turned but of course it was long out of sight. To be honest, she hadn't really seen it to begin with.

He reached for her hand again and she braced herself for the contact. As of the last ten years hadn't happened, his mere touch was enough to send tingles to her toes.

This is not good.

Ryan Beck was a dangerous man.

RYAN HAD ORDERED bacon, eggs, and toast for himself, and Mariah had ordered a lemon-poppy seed muffin after explaining that she'd already had breakfast with Liza earlier.

"Have you lost your appetite?" he teased. "I've seen you put away two breakfasts many times in the past."

Laughing, she shook her head. "Eating like that isn't a good idea. It's bad enough that all the takeout restaurants within ten miles of my apartment are on a first name basis with me."

"Did you ever learn to cook?"

Mariah's parents had sort of been hippies who had started a health food store chain that had somehow become wildly successful despite them not believing much in capitalism. For her, rebellion had consisted of eating junk food and drinking soda. Her parents had put it down to Mariah expressing herself and they'd assumed she'd grow out of it. Apparently, she hadn't.

"No, but I keep telling myself that someday I will. Mom keeps threatening to try and teach me."

That wasn't a good idea either. Mariah's mother was an amazing woman and Ryan adored her but she couldn't cook. Her idea of *cooking* was wheat germ wraps with hummus and sunflower seeds.

A thought popped into Ryan's head and the words were out before he could stop himself.

"Didn't your husband ever want a home-cooked meal?"

Shit. I need to learn to keep my big mouth shut.

Ryan had never met Mariah's ex-husband, but that didn't stop him from wondering about the guy. He didn't even know what he looked like. Liza had offered several times to show him pictures on her phone of the "happy couple" but he'd refused every damn time.

Instead of looking pissed off about his question, Mariah instead appeared confused.

"He was a Michelin star chef, Ryan, so…no. He never expected me to cook at all."

A fucking chef? Leave it Mariah, a food lover, to marry a chef.

"I didn't realize. I guess Liza never told me."

She may have tried but he had ignored her.

Mariah's expression was still quizzical.

"We're divorced now so it doesn't really matter. So how about this apology you promised me? I'm waiting anxiously, although I've been checking the sky carefully."

He followed her gaze out of the restaurant front window to the blue sky overhead. "Why are you checking the weather?"

"I'm not checking the weather. I'm checking for pigs flying."

"Are you referring to my apology?"

She was being more than a bit dramatic about it. He was going to apologize. She deserved one.

"The one I haven't received yet? Yes."

Smart ass.

"I was just waiting until I'd had my coffee but since you're so anxious I can do it now. I'm sorry. I apologize about the way I acted last night. I was a jerk."

She studied him for a long moment and then nodded. "I'm sorry, too. I shouldn't have reacted the way I did. This whole thing with Brad has me off-kilter. And thank you for apologizing."

"You keep saying that I never have before."

"And you think that's wrong."

He frowned, his mind all the way back to when they were dating. "I'm sure that I have. I can't remember a particular instance, but I can't imagine that we went out for years and I never apologized for something in that time."

The waitress slipped his plate in front of him and then set down Mariah's muffin.

"I don't want to start another argument with you, Ryan. The past is the past. Digging it up and examining it won't change anything. But I am sorry for saying that you didn't change. Clearly, you have changed."

"For the better?"

Now, why did I ask that? Do I really want to know?

Laughing, she cut into her muffin. "Does your ego need a boost? Yes, for the better. So far, anyway. You could be a total dick, though, and I just haven't seen it yet."

"I'm not a dick. And I do want to be friends."

He'd thought about it all last night because he had insomnia and didn't sleep much. Mariah. The past. Their argument. And the future too. She was right that them being friends would be easier on Liza, and he wanted to make his sister's life easier if he could. She was the one person in his family that he was still close to.

Her gaze softened and she smiled, a real one. Perhaps the first real smile he'd seen from her since she'd opened her front door last night. He wasn't sure that he liked the way it made his heart lurch and his stomach twist in his gut. He shouldn't be reacting this way at all.

"I'd like that, too."

Clearing this throat, he dug into his breakfast, wanting to ignore the rush of emotion he'd felt. It was out of place. Inconvenient. Unwanted.

"Are you going to the memorial service later?" she asked. "We could split an Uber."

"That's a good idea," he heard himself saying. "We have to be there by three."

"I'll be ready. I won't make you wait."

He opened his mouth to remind her of all the times she had made him wait but then decided it was a bad idea. They were spending way too much time in the history of their relationship.

She believed that he'd changed. He could do the same.

He told himself that he wouldn't think about the past anymore but he knew it was a big lie. This case was dragging him back there whether he liked it or not.

CHAPTER TEN

THEY WERE GOING to give it a second try at being friends. Mariah wasn't sure what changed Ryan's tune this morning but she was happy about it. She hadn't liked that they could barely be around one another. It was hard on Liza and that wasn't fair to her either.

When they'd broken up, it hadn't been some big dramatic thing with lots of crying and yelling. Ryan had brought up the subject first but she hadn't been surprised. They'd been working their way towards it for awhile. If anything, it had sort of been a relief. She didn't have to keep trying so hard anymore. Their relationship had turned into a great deal of work and they'd been too young to know how to do it.

Now that she was older and wiser it didn't look all that daunting, to be honest, but back then their issues had seemed insurmountable.

And actually kind of petty too, when compared to what was happening right now. She was sitting in the pew of a lovely old church listening to the clergyman talk about how wonderful of a person Brad was and how much everyone missed him.

Ryan was sitting next to her, his wide shoulders pressed closely to hers with Liza and her husband Mike on her other side. A few rows in front of them were Jack and Patricia, Ryan and Liza's parents along with Skip and Lily Harrington. Skip's face was stoic, almost carved from granite while Lily cried into a handkerchief as Patricia comforted her. Jack stared straight ahead, his hands folded on his lap and the small program they'd been given when arriving tucked into the breast pocket of his dark suit.

Brad's brother Sebastian was sitting to the left of his father with a pretty woman that appeared to be his girlfriend or maybe wife. Mariah hadn't heard that Seb had married but it was entirely possible. He had his arm around the woman's shoulders and she was sniffling into a shredded tissue while he patted her arm.

The room was full of people that Mariah recognized and a few that she didn't. It was like jumping into the deep end of her past seeing them again. These last several years she hadn't really kept up with most of them, preferring to live a quiet life with her art and a few friends and family.

When the minister finished, Daniel Bosworth went to the podium to talk about Brad. Dan was an old friend and he and Brad had always been close. They'd gone to the same boarding school and then college. They'd been like brothers.

Dan told the assembled guests a few crazy stories from their time at boarding school that had everyone smiling. He ended his speech in tears, his hand over his heart.

"I miss you every day, buddy, and I think of you every day. Rest in peace. You were just too good for this world."

When the service was over, they all filed outside where people were still milling about, hugging and talking.

"Brace yourself," Ryan warned, his hand on her elbow. "Jack and Patricia are heading right for us."

Mariah had always liked Ryan's parents and they'd gotten along well. She understood his frustration with them as they had some very definite ideas about what their son should have done with this career, but she'd never understood the ruthless way he'd basically cut them from his life after college. From what Liza had told her, he barely visited once a year and even then, he avoided his mother and father like the plague. Liza had said that their mother was heartbroken and his father was obviously disappointed, although he hadn't expressed anything out loud.

Jack Beck was an older version of Ryan except with silver hair and a few more lines in his face. Still handsome and vital in his sixties, Jack looked every inch the debonair businessman in his dark pinstriped suit.

Patricia was tall and graceful, her blonde hair cut into a sleek bob that just touched her shoulders. Today she was in a stylish dark blue Chanel suit paired with a simple strand of pearls. She might be sixty in a few days but she could have easily passed for forty-five.

After hugging Ryan, Patricia beamed at Mariah, giving her a kiss on each cheek. "We don't get to see enough of you, dear. You must come by for dinner sometime. I'll call you and set something up."

"I'd love that. I think the last time I saw you was at Liza's birthday party."

The older woman nodded in agreement. "I think that's when it was. Far too long, if you ask me."

"Son," Jack said gruffly, shaking his son's hand before turning to Mariah. "It's wonderful to see you again, Mariah. Patricia is right, you need to come for dinner. In fact, why don't you come with Ryan tomorrow night?"

She could feel Ryan stiffen beside her and she held her breath. This could go so badly or it could be fine.

"Dad, I'm not sure–"

"It would hurt your mother's feelings if you declined," Jack said firmly, his gaze intent on Ryan. "Besides, you have to eat even if you're working."

"We would love to have both of you," Patricia said softly. She was looking at her son with such love and adoration. How did Ryan not see it? "I can have the cook make roast chicken. It's your favorite."

Clearing his throat, Ryan shifted on his feet. "Of course, I'll be there, Mom."

His mother's gaze traveled back to Mariah. "And Mariah, too? We haven't seen her in so long."

"If she's free. I can't speak for her."

It was pure instinct for Mariah to agree. She'd run interference for Ryan with his parents many times before. It came as naturally as breathing. She'd already said yes before she remembered that it wasn't really her problem anymore.

Oh well. The roast chicken is divine.

Jack checked his watch. "We need to be going. I have a conference call with California in an hour."

Patricia hugged Ryan again and the older couple headed for the exit, only stopping to bid goodbye to a few friends.

"Heaven forbid Dad might miss a conference call."

Mariah didn't like the sarcasm in Ryan's tone. It wasn't her job to call him on it anymore but what the hell? Somebody ought to and Liza wasn't here to do it.

"What's your problem? He has a conference call. So what?"

"He always put work before his family."

"His family seems fine today. Why is it so terrible that he might take a call? You worked today, too."

A muscle jumped in his cheek. She'd pissed him off. Good.

"That wasn't a big deal."

"Maybe this call isn't either."

"Whose side are you on?"

"Is it a war? Call me Switzerland."

"You know how he is."

"I do, but I don't think you do."

He muttered something under his breath that she couldn't quite make out but had the feeling it wasn't all that complimentary of her. She had a few things she could say right back to him.

With his hand on her lower back, he pressed her forward toward the exit but immediately their path was blocked by one of their old friends, Carl Winwood.

"We're all going to have a drink," Carl said, giving Mariah a hug. "You have to come, too."

Carl had been Ryan's best friend for years. Red-haired and freckled, Carl always had a big smile on his face except for today. Did they still keep in touch? She had no idea, but she'd always liked him. He'd brought out the best in Ryan and vice versa.

Raising his brows in question, Ryan waited for her to accept or decline. She would say yes, of course. She wanted to see her old friends and catch up, although it was a terrible reason for a reunion.

They all decided to meet up at a restaurant and bar within walking distance. Ryan and Mariah walked with Carl and he'd assured them that most of the group was already there. Without spouses. It was just going to be the old friend group today.

"It's awful that we're seeing each other under these sad circumstances but I'm so damn glad to see both of you," Carl said as he pulled open the door of the bar. "We can't let it go this long again."

"We won't," Ryan promised, clapping his friend on the shoulder. "I've been too caught up in my job but I want to change that. Make time for my friends more."

Mariah didn't say much as they were led deeper into the restaurant to a back area that was dimly lit and quiet, separate from the rest of the establishment with a set of French doors. Two tables had been pushed together and most of the chairs were already filled with familiar faces.

Dan was there, as was Theo Perkins, both dressed in dark

suits but there the similarity ended. Dan looked like a blond surfer guy while Theo had the dark hair and eyes passed down from his Greek grandmother.

Liza and her husband Mike were there too, of course. Liza was talking to Daphne Eastman and Isla Norton. On her other side was Trent Garfield, tapping something out on his phone and barely giving the group any of his attention.

Trent had a love-hate thing going with Brad all those years ago. They were friends but deeply competitive with one another. They competed about anything and everything. Cars, grades, women, or something as stupid as who could eat the most cheeseburgers. They'd constantly tried to one up each other and most of the time it had been a friendly sort of thing. But a few days before Brad's disappearance they'd argued – loudly. Trent had stomped off and Mariah had no idea if they'd ever made up. Trent hadn't been at the bar the night Brad had disappeared.

"Where is—"

Mariah didn't finish her question. The answer had just walked into the room. The one person she hadn't seen yet.

Caroline – red-faced and crying. Her eyes were swollen from tears. She and Brad had dated on and off for years, although she'd married Dan about eight years ago. From what Mariah had heard, Dan and Caroline had two kids and were very happy together.

"Oh my God, Mariah! I'm so glad to see you!"

Caroline rushed forward and wrapped Mariah in a hug before stepping back, her gaze darting back and forth between

Ryan and her friend.

"Are you two back together? That's wonderful," she gushed. "Finally, some good news. I always knew you two were meant for each other. You look amazing together. Like it was meant to be. True love."

Well…dammit.

Mariah didn't want to rain on Caroline's parade, especially on a day like today, but she didn't want everyone thinking that she and Ryan were back together. They weren't. The friends thing was hard enough.

"Um, we're just here as friends," Mariah replied, stumbling a little over the words. "It's not like…that."

"Just friends," Ryan piped up, his hand squeezing her elbow slightly as if he was nervous. "But good friends."

She'd been promoted to *good* friend today. That was fast.

"Oh." Caroline's face fell. "That's okay, I guess."

Dan had stood when his wife entered the room and came up beside Caroline, sliding his arm around her waist. "Honey, if you need to go home I can call you–"

"No," the other woman said with a firm shake of her head. "I want to be here with all of my friends. I'm not going home."

Pivoting on her high heel, Caroline strode to the table and sat down in an empty chair, signaling the waitress. Dan watched and then turned back to Ryan and Mariah, his expression concerned.

"I'm worried about her. She keeps saying that she's fine but she's been crying on and off since we got the news. I think she's afraid that I'll be angry if she reveals just how upset she is about all of this. Hell, we're all upset. Why shouldn't she be, too? She and Brad were together for a long time. I wouldn't expect anything less."

"That's a good attitude to have," Ryan said. "Just let her know that you're there for her. It'll be alright eventually."

Dan nodded, his solemn gaze resting on Mariah. "I heard about your divorce. I'm sorry we didn't get in touch. We've been terrible friends."

She shook her head. "No, it's fine. Really."

"Still–" Dan broke off and then shrugged. "No excuses. We should have done better."

The three of them stood there awkwardly for a moment before Dan nodded toward the group. It was weird to be with people that knew each other so well but now didn't have much to say to one another. A wall of tension had suddenly appeared out of nowhere, making it even stranger than Mariah had expected.

"Come and sit down. Order a drink. We're going to toast Brad."

To her surprise, Ryan took her hand and she relaxed almost immediately. It felt warm and reassuring, strong when she felt weak and unsure. That was one good thing about Ryan Beck. He rarely felt unsure about anything. He was always completely confident that he was right. She'd loved that about him. And hated it, too.

"Are you ready?" he asked softly as they made their way to

the table. "Give me the signal if you need to get out of here."

He'd remembered. They had a "signal" that they'd use when she'd had enough of people and parties. He was far more extroverted than she was, although as she'd grown older she'd learned how to pretend.

"I'm fine. It's all fine."

It would be. These were her friends – or at least they had been. They'd catch up and pretend that they'd stay in touch more. Hug and exchange phone numbers and social media. In the end, probably not much would change. Everyone was busy living their life.

Everyone but Brad, and that's why they were there.

CHAPTER ELEVEN

RYAN'S FRIEND GROUP had changed quite a bit since they were in college, but in some ways, nothing had changed at all. Carl was still quiet, only speaking when he had something to say; Trent was boisterous and loud, even though this wasn't a party. He kept answering his phone and speaking loudly to someone that clearly worked for him. Ryan would have quit his job if his boss talked to him that way.

Dan was reminiscing about Brad, seemingly unaware of Caroline crying softly next to him. Every story only served to make his wife more upset. She was currently finding solace with Daphne, who was the softest touch of their group. Daphne had always been the "den mother" that reminded the more irresponsible ones that they needed to get some sleep or study.

Isla was a talker as well and she liked to hear the sound of her own voice, apparently, because she'd barely taken a breath since she'd started on her second cocktail. She was telling Mariah about her husband, kids, and the chain of day spas she owned.

Theo, as usual, was more focused on the pretty waitresses than on the conversation. His head had whipped around several times already to catch a glimpse of a retreating server's shapely rear end.

Liza and Mike were talking to Carl about their trip to Europe last year. Carl had visited Prague just a few weeks ago and was talking about the incredible food.

And Mariah? She was listening to Isla politely, nodding and responding in all the right places which surprised Ryan. Isla and Mariah had never gotten on back in the day. Isla had often made fun of Mariah, calling her old-fashioned and a prude because she'd stuck with Ryan while Isla wanted to sow her wild oats while she was young. She didn't think it was healthy for a young woman to commit herself to one man before she was thirty. It appeared she hadn't taken her own advice.

To be honest, Ryan hadn't liked to be around Isla either. She was often difficult to be with as she was quite opinionated and liked to argue. Then when she'd pissed you off thoroughly and frustrated the hell out of you, she would simply laugh and say she was just playing devil's advocate and that you shouldn't take things so seriously.

"Dude, you've barely said a word." Carl elbowed Ryan to get his attention. Isla had turned her attention to Liza and Mike. "Earth to Ryan."

He had spaced out a little. His mind was going a mile a minute. He needed to talk to these people about that night. About Brad and what they might know about what was going on in their friend's life at the time, but he needed to do it separately. Not as a group. He also didn't want to ruin the vibe of this get-together. This was about remembering Brad.

But Ryan had a job to do and finding out what happened that night would bring closure to many people. This group included.

"I was thinking about how much we've changed yet some things always stay the same."

"We have bigger bank accounts but who we are as people probably hasn't changed much." He nodded toward Trent, who had finally hung up his phone and was regaling Theo with a tale about the time he'd beat Brad at basketball. "Some things never change. Still trying to outdo Brad and he isn't even here to compete with. He wants to be the center of attention at a wake, for fuck's sake. How needy is that?"

"Do you remember what he and Brad fought about a few days before?"

"No, but I assume it was something trivial because, let's face it, it always was. I do remember Brad saying that he wished Trent wasn't going on the Hawaii trip with us but I didn't pay any attention to it. They talked shit about each other all the time, but when the chips were down, they were there for each other." Carl's brows rose slowly. "Wait...you don't think? Not Trent. He wouldn't do something like that. No way. He's one of us. I mean, he's kind of an asshole but he wouldn't actually hurt anyone."

This was what Ryan had been worried about. He wasn't here to accuse anyone. He simply needed to know what had been going on in Brad's life the few weeks before his disappearance.

He was, however, afraid that his friends might "circle the wagons" and stay silent on an important piece of information.

"I'm not saying that Trent did anything," Ryan explained. "I'm just hoping that one of us might know what Brad was doing and who he was hanging out with. Maybe Trent argued with Brad about someone else? I need to know that. You probably don't know this but I'm helping Brad's family investigate what happened to him."

"*Everybody* knows that. We're counting on you to find out the truth."

"Everybody?" Ryan echoed. "How could everyone know? I barely got into town yesterday."

Carl shrugged. "Skip and Lily told Theo's parents who told mine or something like that. Does it matter? We all know, and we're all glad that you're doing this. It was lucky you became a cop. I wouldn't be much help on something like this."

His friend was a mergers and acquisitions specialist. Carl traveled a great deal and had recently split from his wife, but they were working on getting back together in couples therapy.

"So do you?" Ryan asked again. "Do you know what Trent and Brad fought about? Or do you know what Brad had going on right before he disappeared? Was he hanging around with anyone new? Did he talk about anything?"

Shrugging again, Carl fidgeted in his chair. "Shit, I don't know. Brad was yelling that Trent was a cheat, and Trent was saying that Brad didn't know what he was talking about. I assumed they had made a bet and Trent wasn't keeping his end of it. You know how they were. Friends one minute and enemies the next. It was no big deal. As for what Brad was doing, I don't know. That last year he didn't talk to me as much. He was always closer to Theo and Dan. They'd know what Brad had going on."

That was true. While they were all a group of friends, some were closer than others. Brad and Ryan had definitely not been as close as they had in the past.

"I'm going to talk to both of them. I'm going to talk to everyone, actually." Ryan paused, wanting to phrase the next question just the right way. "Was Brad…seeing anyone that you know of?"

Carl gave him a shrewd look. "You mean besides Caro?"

"That's what I mean. We both know…"

Ryan didn't have to spell it out. Everyone had known that Brad ran around behind Caroline's back.

Sadly, she'd known it, too.

Carl's gaze darted to Isla and then back. It was fast but Ryan had caught it.

"Isla? He was seeing her?"

"He didn't care about her or anything, he was just…you know…having some fun. She was up for it. I don't think she was in love with him or anything."

"Brad acted like she wasn't all that attractive. He said she was too obvious."

"Sometimes he liked them obvious," Carl whispered. "They kind of hated each other but from what I gather the sex was hot.

He said she was pretty wild in the sack."

"When did he say this? Where was I?"

Chuckling, Carl grinned. "With Mariah, where you always were. We were playing golf a few days before leaving for Hawaii. You hated golf."

"I still hate golf."

"That's why you weren't there."

Isla and Brad. Interesting couple.

"How long had he been seeing her?"

"I have no idea and I wouldn't even call it *seeing* her. They were...having sex. That's it. More like enemies with benefits, if you ask me. I doubt he hung around afterward and cuddled and talked."

"Did Caro know?"

"I don't think so, but I could be wrong. She never said anything to me about it. She might have said something to Mariah."

"Mariah would have told me if she had."

Ryan was sure of it. They'd told each other everything.

"So...you and Mariah. I didn't think I'd ever see you two together again."

"It's not like that."

His answer was reflexive and swift. His friend group loved a little gossip. For the most part, he'd managed not to be a focus of it.

Carl scratched his chin. "Why not? She's single again and you both clearly still have feelings for each other."

"Why do you think that? We're just friends."

And barely that. Basically, they'd called a truce this morning. They were hardly texting each other and making lunch plans.

"Because you've barely taken your eyes off of her since you walked into the memorial service. And the same for her. You can't deny that Mariah is one gorgeous woman. Hell, I'd be looking at her too if I wasn't trying to fix my marriage."

"We're just friends."

He was going to have to watch his behavior much more closely because people might get the wrong idea. If he was watching Mariah, it wasn't because he wanted to start something between them. It was because…

Fuck it. He didn't have to explain himself to anyone. In fact, Carl was probably just busting Ryan's balls about Mariah. He probably wasn't even looking at her at all.

Carl held up his hands in surrender. "Okay, if you say so. I was just saying that you could do worse. She's beautiful and she's always been terrific. Everyone thinks she's great."

"Listen, it's okay," Ryan said with a sigh, trying to relax. He'd been too wound up today. "I'm just feeling the pressure about this investigation. I want to do right by Brad and his family."

"You will," Carl assured him. "You're a badass cop. I tell all of my friends and co-workers about you. We're all proud as hell of you."

If only Ryan's family felt that way.

"Thanks, but I'm just doing my job. Just like you."

Chuckling, Carl shook his head. "I don't get to do anything

exciting or dangerous. In fact, my life is boring as hell while you're out catching bad guys."

"It's not like it looks in the movies. Trust me. I spend a lot of my time in the office doing research."

Carl didn't look like he believed Ryan.

"So do you have any leads on what happened to Brad? Any theories?"

None that Ryan wanted to talk about so he tried to joke his way out of the question. His friends probably didn't know about the medical examiner's report yet.

"Hey, give me a break. I just got here yesterday. I haven't even unpacked yet. I have a lot of people to talk to."

His friend wasn't the pushy type so he thankfully let it go.

"Just know that we're all rooting for you. We know you'll figure out what happened to Brad."

It wouldn't be easy. Cold cases never were.

Brad, what did you do that night? What was going on in your life?

★ ★ ★

AT ONE POINT, Mariah and Caroline had been close friends. During their teenage years, they'd spent the night at each other's house and talked about what their lives were going to be like when they were grown up. Caroline had wanted to get married and have kids, and so did Mariah, although in her fantasies she was also a celebrated artist.

One out of three isn't too bad. And I'm still young.

Okay, point-five out of three. I can't call myself celebrated but I do make a living at it.

After going to different universities they'd drifted apart slightly. Still friends, but not the kind that divulged deep secrets to one another. They'd mostly partied together with the rest of the group. Caroline had been dating Brad, and Mariah was with Ryan. Brad and Ryan were friends too, so they all seem to end up in the same places on a regular basis. She got along with Caroline and they'd never argued, but later when Mariah and Ryan ended things, somehow she hadn't heard from Caroline anymore.

To be honest, Caroline had started separating herself from the group after Brad's disappearance. It had been a huge surprise when she'd married Dan, but she'd been absolutely radiant at the wedding and Mariah was thrilled that she'd found love after all that had happened.

Mariah had let Daphne and Caroline do most of the talking but eventually the conversation wound around to her life and what she was doing with it.

"You and Ryan look good together," Daphne said. "Do you still feel any of the old tingles? Maybe you guys could give it another shot. You're single again."

Tingles? My heart races and my palms get sweaty. But I'll never admit it.

"We're just friends. His apartment is across the hall from mine so we shared a taxi here. It's not a big deal."

Daphne looked over Mariah's shoulder to where Ryan was

deep in conversation with Carl.

"He still looks good. Even better, actually. The cop stuff is kind of...manly, too. Not like my husband who sits behind a desk all day and then plays golf on Saturdays."

Mariah wasn't sure what Ryan was doing to stay in shape but it was working well. If anything, he was in better condition than when they were in school.

"I'm not looking for a relationship right now."

Caroline frowned. "You want to be alone forever?"

"Not forever, just...for now. Relationships are a lot of work. I'm just enjoying dating and my work. I'm not looking to take care of a man."

Mariah's ex-husband had been high maintenance to say the least, and by the time they'd divorced she'd been exhausted trying to keep him happy. Eventually she'd had to admit that it was a goal that was never going to be achieved. Bobby was never happy and she didn't think he wanted to be either.

"I don't like to think of you alone," Caroline pressed. "Do you have a cat or a dog?"

"I'm thinking of getting a cat." She waved away their concern. "I'm fine. Honest. I'm just glad to see both of you. It's been so long."

Welling up with tears again, Caroline sniffled. "I love both of you so much but I hate that we're together because of Brad's death. I guess I fooled myself into believing that he was really alive all of this time. You know, he used to talk about faking his death. Do you remember? He said he'd go off to some tropical island and sell fishing gear to tourists. I didn't want to think anything bad happened to him so I would imagine that he was there."

"I heard him say it more than once," Daphne said. "I didn't take him seriously. I assumed it was a joke."

"I'm sure it was a joke," Caroline replied, her eyes watery. "But it made me feel better, if that makes any sense. Now I can't pretend that he isn't gone."

"When did you last talk to Brad?" Mariah asked. "What did he say?"

"He said he wanted to stay and drink some more with Theo. He told me he'd meet me at the airport the next morning. I told him that we should both go home but you know how he was, stubborn as a mule. He wanted to stay so there was no point in arguing with him."

"And you didn't hear from him after that?"

"No, but I didn't expect to. I went home and went to bed. When we got to the airport, he wasn't there. But you know that."

Caroline had been livid when Brad hadn't shown up that day. Absolutely furious. She'd tried to call him a dozen times at least while they waited to board the plane. She'd been pissed off during the entire flight but had finally settled down when they'd landed, deciding to enjoy the trip without Brad.

Sniffling and dabbing at her eyes with a tissue, Caroline stood from her chair. "I'm going to the ladies' room to try and fix my eyeliner. I'll be right back. Will you order me another martini?"

When Caroline turned the corner and was out of sight, Daphne leaned closer to Mariah.

"She was cheating on Brad. I think that's why she's so upset. She feels guilty."

This was news to Mariah. She'd never even suspected.

"Cheating? Are you sure?"

Daphne nodded toward Trent, who was talking to Ryan. "With him. She told me. She was mad at Brad for running around and not paying enough attention to her so she was sleeping with Trent. When we were in Hawaii, I saw her sneak into his hotel room when she thought the rest of us were asleep."

"What were you doing up?"

Smiling even wider, Daphne waggled her eyebrows. "I was sneaking into Theo's room."

"How did I not know any of this?"

"There was a lot of sleeping around back then but you and Ryan weren't a part of that. We didn't hide it from you, but we didn't shout about it either. Honestly, I think you just wanted to think the best of everyone, so even if you had seen me sneak into Theo's room, would you have thought I was doing it to have sex with him?"

Was I that naive back then?

"I wasn't a prude or anything. I wouldn't have judged you."

"I know. You're not that type." Daphne's gaze moved to Caroline's husband Dan at the end of the table. "I don't think Danny knows about Trent, so let's just keep that between us, okay? It was a long time ago and it doesn't really matter anymore, right?"

"Right. I won't say anything to him." Mariah wasn't so sure that it didn't matter anymore, however. "Did Brad know about Caro and Trent?"

Daphne's eyes went round and she shook her head. "No way. He would have killed Trent."

"They were arguing a few days before he disappeared. And he was kind of nasty to Caro that night. Are you sure he didn't know?"

"Well...I don't think so. Brad would have been livid. He wasn't an equal opportunity cheater, if you know what I mean. It was one thing for him to chase girls but he would have gone ballistic if he thought Caroline was doing the same thing. No, I don't think he knew. It would have been ugly if he did."

It *had* been ugly. A young man had lost his life that night. Was Trent involved? Or Caroline?

Mariah's gaze swept over her old friends just sitting and chatting with one another. Was one of them responsible for Brad's death? She didn't want to think about that possibility, but she couldn't shake the idea.

What if it wasn't a stranger? What if it was someone she knew?

CHAPTER TWELVE

R YAN HAD MADE plans for the next day to meet up with the other friends in the group that he hadn't had a chance to speak with. He needed to talk to all of them about that night. Already he'd found out that Brad was cheating on Caroline with Isla. What else didn't he know?

It wasn't that he thought that Isla had killed Brad, hitting him on the head, but if Ryan didn't know about their covert relationship there might be a hell of a lot more that he didn't know about Brad's life. Important details that might lead to solving the mystery of what happened that night.

"Caroline was sleeping with Trent."

Ryan and Mariah had just exited the Uber vehicle and were walking into the apartment building.

"Hold that thought."

He punched the elevator button and the doors dinged and then slid open. He urged Mariah inside and the doors closed.

"Can you say that again?"

"Caroline was sleeping with Trent. Daphne told me today. She said that Caroline told her all those years ago, and she also saw Caroline sneaking into Trent's hotel room in Hawaii. Did you know Daphne was sleeping with Theo?"

That was two pieces of information. Neither one he was aware of.

"No, I didn't know about Daphne and Theo but I'm not really all that surprised. They were constantly flirting with one another. I would have been more surprised if something hadn't happened, to be honest. Now let's get back to Caroline and Trent. How long was that going on?"

"I don't know. Daphne just said that Caro was angry about Brad running around on her and being a dick so she was getting back at him by sleeping with Trent."

It was the perfect revenge since Trent and Brad were *frenemies*, always competing with one another. Trent would have loved to tell Brad that he'd slept with Caroline.

"And Brad knew?"

Mariah shook her head. "Daphne says that he didn't."

The doors slid open and they headed down the hall. He didn't reply until Mariah had unlocked her door and they were in her apartment.

"I find that hard to believe. If Trent slept with Caroline, he'd want Brad to know. He'd enjoy telling the news. In fact, I'm surprised he didn't tell all of us with a PowerPoint presentation. It would have been the ultimate fuck-you-I'm-better to Brad."

"Daphne was sure that Brad didn't know. She said that he'd be livid if he found out and I have to agree with that. Think about what you said as well. If Trent had told Brad, he would have told all of us. He didn't. So I think that Daphne may be right that no one else knew."

It didn't make sense to Ryan, not with what he knew about the two men.

"Are you saying that Trent had *feelings* for Caroline then? Because that would shock the hell out of me. He never seemed to even like her very much. He sure as hell didn't have any patience for her."

"He didn't have patience with anyone," Mariah pointed out. "Let's face it, Trent was kind of an asshole. If he hadn't been a childhood friend of yours would you have been hanging out with him?"

"He was always that way."

"That's not a great excuse for being a jerk."

"Trent isn't that bad. He'd give you the shirt off his back if you needed it."

"And then tell everyone that he did it."

Maybe. Probably. The fact was Trent had all sorts of issues. He'd had a fucked-up childhood, being shuttled from one neglectful parent to the other, and mostly been brought up by nannies and housekeepers. Freud would have had a field day with the guy and his need to be loved and admired.

Mariah sat down on the couch, stretching out her legs and kicking off her high heels. He'd forgotten just how gorgeous her legs were. She used to run to keep them toned. Did she still do that? It looked like it. They were also tanned from the summer sun.

Shit, is it hot in here?

"Ryan," she said sharply, pulling him from his daydreams. "Did you hear me? I said, do you think that's what Trent and Brad argued about?"

Pull it together, man. They're just legs. Attached to Mariah.

"I don't know. I'm going to talk to Trent tomorrow. I didn't have a chance tonight."

"He may not tell you the truth."

"I like to think that I know when someone is lying."

Her brow quirked up. "You have that superpower? Lucky you."

"People have tells when they lie."

"Can you tell if I'm lying?"

Chuckling, Ryan nodded. "Yes, you rub your earlobe when you're telling a fib."

"That's not true," she said with a scowl. "I don't do that. And when have I ever lied to you?"

"I said a fib, not a lie. Remember when my sister was dating that guy from Stanford that I couldn't stand? Shit, I can't even remember his name now but he was a jerk. She went out on a date with him and you told me she was out with her friends. She didn't want me to know because she knew I'd give her a hard time about it. You covered for her."

"Of course I did, she's my best friend."

"And you rubbed your earlobe when you did it."

Her expression was scandalized as her hand flew up to her ear. "So you knew I was lying?"

"Not then, but later when I was being trained, I thought back to that. You've done it more than a few times. Like when you told me that you liked camping and the show 'Lost'."

"I was trying to impress you. I never thought we would actually go camping, and I didn't think you'd make such a big deal about a television show."

"It was one of my favorites."

"We both liked 'The Sopranos'."

"You liked 'American Idol'. Admit it."

"Millions of people liked 'American Idol'. I won't apologize for it, Ryan. Here we go again. Even your taste in television shows has to be superior to everyone else's. Get over yourself."

"I'm just saying that some shows and movies are better than others."

Rolling her eyes, she walked over to the refrigerator and pulled out two water bottles, handing one to him.

"I'm saying that I don't care what other people watch or read or sing or do. It's none of my business."

To be perfectly honest, Ryan wasn't sure why he cared what Mariah watched or liked. Maybe because he'd found her so fascinating back then, or perhaps because he'd wanted her to like the same things he did. Her approval had been important to him when he was younger.

"According to Carl, Brad was sleeping with Isla."

Mariah's mouth fell open in shock. "Wait…what? Brad and Isla? How does Carl know? And how didn't you know?"

"Brad and I weren't that close, and personally, I didn't want to hear about his sexual exploits, most of which I assumed were lies. Carl swears it's true, though, and that Brad told him."

"I'm not sure that I believe it."

"Why not?"

"You said it. Brad lied about stuff. I can see him lying about Isla."

Sitting down on the couch, Ryan re-ran Carl's words through his head one more time.

"Carl seemed pretty convinced it was true. I didn't question it but I probably should have. I'm going to have to ask Isla."

Mariah held up her hand in a stop motion. "Why would you ask her? What does it matter?"

"For the same reason it matters that Caroline was sleeping with Trent."

She was shaking her head before he'd finished answering. "No, it matters because Brad would have been jealous if he knew and that might be why they argued."

"Caroline could be jealous, too."

"She might but she knew that Brad ran around all the time. She'd never killed him over it. Past performance is the best predictor of future behavior. If she didn't kill him before, why would she do it now?"

"Maybe Isla was the straw that broke the camel's back? He was fishing in our friend group pond, so to speak, and she was angry."

"Except that she was sleeping with Trent," Mariah reminded him. "So why would she be mad? She was getting her revenge.

She didn't need to kill him."

He'd been thinking about the whole situation. In fact, that was pretty much all he was doing.

When he wasn't thinking about Mariah, that is.

"What if it was a tragic accident? They argued. Things got heated. Maybe Brad took a swing at Caro and she was defending herself? Or he was arguing with Trent and it got physical? It doesn't have to be premeditated cold-blooded murder."

"So you do have theories?"

"I have theories and hardly any evidence, so they don't mean much. At this point I'm just running scenarios through my head to see if they make any sense. Let's face it, anything could have happened. Brad liked to run his mouth when he was drinking and he could have pissed off the wrong person that night."

Mariah sat down next to Ryan. "I know that you know what you're doing with this investigation, but be honest with me. Just what are the chances of you finding out what really happened to Brad that night?"

"The more time has passed from the crime, the harder it is to solve the mystery," Ryan explained. "Memories fade, witnesses disappear or die. Evidence goes missing or degrades. About forty percent of homicides are never solved. Cold cases have the best chance of being solved when there is evidence that can be used with more modern investigative techniques like DNA analysis."

"That's a fancy way of saying that this is a long shot," Mariah replied softly. "You have very little evidence and no motive."

"That we know of. Someone definitely had means and opportunity. My job is to find out all of Brad's secrets. We've already uncovered two. Maybe one of them will lead us to the truth."

Something bad had happened to Brad that night. Ryan was determined to find out what.

And who.

CHAPTER THIRTEEN

T HE NEXT MORNING Ryan was standing in Theo Perkins' palatial office. Situated on an upper floor, it had an impressive view of downtown Chicago, which was what Ryan studied while he waited for his old friend to finish a phone call. Theo had gone into his father's law firm, a business that had been in the family for generations.

Hanging up the phone, Theo whirled around in his leather chair and gave Ryan a huge grin.

"Sorry about that. It never ends around here." He jumped up and headed for the office door. "How about a coffee? I could do with one. Cream and sugar?"

Ryan hadn't yet had his first cup today as he'd been anxious to get up and get started on the investigation. He had several items on his to-do list.

"That would be great. Cream and two sugars."

At home he would have had it black but for some reason now that he was back in Chicago, he was drinking it with cream and sugar again.

Theo stuck his head out of the office and asked his assistant to get them two coffees. Instead of going to sit behind his desk, he sat down on the small sofa against the wall and Ryan followed suit. It was a relief that there wasn't going to be any sort of power plays this morning, but then Theo wasn't really the type for that. He'd always been laid back and relaxed.

"So you want to talk about that night?"

"I'm talking to everyone that I can find that was there that night, especially as Mariah and I left the bar early."

It sounded so natural. *Mariah and I.*

Being friends with her yesterday hadn't been so bad. To be truthful, he'd enjoyed her company. As always, her intelligence and insight impressed him, plus she was easy to be around. Not restful or serene, though. No, she was too challenging for that. But easy in the sense that he always knew where he stood with her. She didn't play head games and that was a relief.

"I'm not sure that I can be much help. That was a long time ago. These days I'm lucky if I can remember that I had for lunch the day before. I'm just so busy these days."

Ryan could completely understand. He'd get so focused on work everything else would fade into the background.

"Let's start at the beginning of the evening. Did Brad say or do anything different than normal? Was he acting strangely?"

Theo shook his head. "No, it was the usual stuff. He was in the mood to cut loose after working so hard the last half of the semester to bring his grades up. His dad had been really on him about that, and Brad had to really buckle down those final weeks. When he came home from school, he'd been on a mission to have some fun so we'd been going out pretty much every single night."

"Was he worried about anything?"

"He wasn't worried about a thing after finals. He was in a great mood."

There was a brief knock and then the door swung open to reveal a young woman holding a tray with two mugs and a basket of pastries.

"Help yourself," Theo said as the assistant placed small plates and napkins on the coffee table in front of them. "There's a bakery about a block down that makes these. They're unbelievably good."

The smell of sugar and vanilla teased Ryan's nostrils and he found himself digging into a still-warm cinnamon roll with cream cheese frosting. So far Chicago had him going back to a hell of a lot of bad habits.

Like Mariah, for instance.

Note to self. You need to go for a long run tonight. Stay away from her.

"So tell me more about that night. We were all doing shots and talking about Hawaii. Then Mariah and I left. What happened after that?"

His brows pinched together, Theo didn't answer immediately. "Shit, I'm not sure. Like I said, that was a long time ago. I think I danced with your sister Liza, and then I went to play pool again. Brad and Caro were talking and drinking but then I think she must have left because Brad was talking with someone else. I'd met a girl that wanted me to teach her to play pool and ended up leaving with her right after they announced last call."

"You didn't go home together?"

With a sheepish grin, Theo shook his head. "What can I say? I got lucky that night."

Ryan couldn't help but think that a best friend disappearing wasn't all that *lucky*. Apparently, the reality of what Theo had said dawned on the other man and the color drained from his face. He'd gone from smiling to almost crying in less than sixty seconds.

"Shit, that didn't come out right. You know what I mean. Of course, I don't think that it was lucky that Brad died. He was my best friend. We were like brothers. I loved him. I really did. If I had known something would happen to him that night...fuck. I never would have left him. I thought he'd be okay. It wasn't the first time one of us went home alone. If he'd met someone, he would have done the same."

When Ryan didn't respond right away, Theo hopped up from the couch and began pacing in front of his desk.

"I know this looks bad. I mean...it's such a coincidence...but I swear that wasn't the only time that he and I went home separately. It happened more often than not because he'd either be going home with Caro or some other girl."

From what Ryan remembered, that was true. But it was a strange coincidence.

"Who else knew you were leaving separately? Were you at the bar when you told him? Could someone have overheard you?"

Pausing in front of the table, Theo stroked his chin. "He was at the bar with some girl. Caro had already left. He told me she was mad and he'd make up with her in the morning. I told him I was leaving and he laughed and told me to have a good time. I don't know if anyone could have overheard us. The music was so loud in there. I guess the girl could have overheard."

"Do you remember her name?"

"No, he didn't mention it and she never said. In fact, I don't remember her saying anything. She was pretty, though. A redhead. Petite. Nice figure."

"Had you seen her before?"

Theo perched on the edge of his desk. "Yeah, I think so. She'd been there a few nights before. She was good-looking, someone you would notice, if you know what I mean. I got the feeling that Brad was planning to go home with her.'"

Ryan made a mental note to somehow try and find out who that woman was, although the odds weren't in his favor.

"So you left? You didn't see him again after that?"

"When I left, he was still at the bar." Theo scraped his fingers through his short brown hair. "That was the last time I saw him alive. It's been years and I still can't believe he's gone. Every now and then I'll reach for my phone to call and tell him some good news."

"What about other girls?" Ryan asked, already knowing part of the answer. "Brad wasn't exactly faithful to Caroline. How many others were there?"

"A few. They didn't mean anything. Brad just wanted to be free and have a good time. He wasn't looking to settle down. Caro could never understand that. She wanted them to get married as soon as they graduated from college. Then have a kid the next year. She had it all planned out. Brad used to tell me about all of her plans. Hell, she'd even picked out the neighborhood she wanted to live in and the car she wanted to drive."

"Why didn't he ever break up with her if she was pressuring him like that?"

"Because he really did love her," Theo said, his expression turning to a frown. "In his way. He didn't want to hurt her, he just wanted her to back off a little bit."

"And how did Isla fit into all of this?"

"She was a fun distraction. Brad said she was wild in the sack. He wasn't in love with her or anything."

"Was she in love with him?"

Theo's brows shot up in surprise. "Fuck, no. If anything, she hated Brad. I swear they were just hate-fucking each other because they both had the same kinks."

Do I even want to know? Not particularly, but it might be important.

"Kinks? Anything dangerous?"

"They both liked threesomes. And four or fivesomes. Shit, is that even a word? Anyway, they liked to make sex a party."

"How did they find this out about each other? I sure as shit don't remember this coming up in casual conversations."

"The way Brad described it, he didn't know either. The

night after he got back into town from school, we saw Isla and Daphne out at The Alleyway. Brad and Isla got drunk and ended up making out. Long story short, he went home with her and she asked if it was okay if the roommate and roommate's boyfriend joined in. Brad was into it, so…"

More names to add to Ryan's list to talk to. Roommate and roommate's boyfriend.

I'm sure they're going to want to unearth some one-night stand from over a decade ago.

"Did Brad and Caro argue a lot about this?"

"She didn't know. She knew he flirted and shit, but she didn't have any idea that Brad was getting his freak on just about every other night with some girl."

Ryan finished the last bite of his cinnamon roll. "She knew. Trust me."

"He never told her."

"He didn't have to. He wasn't exactly discreet. People talk, Theo. Now…were they arguing a lot? Brad had been home from university less than three weeks but it sounds like he'd been a busy boy. Was Caroline pissed about that? She wasn't the happiest person that last night."

Theo's shoulders sagged. "He said that she was riding him hard. Wanted him to straighten up and start making future plans. But I swear, he didn't know that she knew all that he was up to. He always said that Caro would kill him if she'd found out he'd slept with another girl. Wait…you don't think…? No way would Caro do something like this."

"I don't think anything. I'm just trying to figure out what happened that night, and who might have had motive and opportunity. We've always known that Caroline was the jealous type but none of us thought for one single second that she offed Brad after he disappeared."

Ryan didn't tell Theo about Caroline and Trent. One, because he didn't know if it was the actual truth, and two, because it wasn't Theo's business. He was a little surprised that Theo didn't already know. Their social group wasn't known for keeping their mouths shut.

Or was he completely wrong about that? It seemed that some people had secrets that Ryan hadn't known anything about back then. Maybe they weren't the gossipy circle he'd thought they were.

"That's good," Theo replied, relief in his tone. "There's no way Caro would have done something like this. She loved Brad. It took her a long time to move on and it was only because Danny had been there to support her through it all. They were friends first."

"I have to ask this. Did Danny have any feelings for Caroline that you know of? He never mentioned anything to me."

"Not that I know of. He was sort of there for her out of sympathy in the beginning. You know how he is...the kind of guy who would take in a stray kitten. I think he felt sorry for her, to be honest."

"They seem to be very happy now."

"They are. We don't see them much but when we do, they

seem to be really in love and happy together."

Ryan didn't have any more questions, at least not for Theo. He stood and pulled a business card from his pocket, placing it on the coffee table.

"Thank you for meeting me this morning. I have several people to talk to today so I won't take up any more of your time. If you think of anything else, call me. Anything at all. What seems like a small, insignificant detail can often be the missing puzzle piece that breaks a case open."

Chuckling, Theo picked up the card and tucked it in his breast pocket. "It's kind of strange, you being a cop. I know you talked about it all the time, but to be honest, I think we all thought you'd give in and go into business with your dad. But here you are…a cop. You did it. Just like you promised."

"I was never going to go into the family business."

"That's what Mariah always said but I have to admit that we didn't believe her. I guess she was right."

Mariah had said so? He hadn't known that.

Maybe she'd known him a little better than he'd given her credit for.

"I hope you find out the truth about what happened that night," Theo continued. "We're all counting on you to solve this and figure out who or what killed Brad."

That's exactly what Ryan planned to do. Next stop…Caroline and Daniel Bosworth.

CHAPTER FOURTEEN

M ARIAH AND DAPHNE had promised to visit Caroline the next day. They'd planned to catch up on each other's lives but in reality, it was about supporting Caroline in her grief. She was taking Brad's death hard and they wanted to be there for her even if they hadn't been all that close in the last ten years.

Since the day was warm and sunny, they'd decided to sit out next to the pool. Caroline and Dan had a large, beautiful home in an affluent suburb for their family of four, plus a cute beagle named Ted. The children – a boy named Adam and a girl named Alice – were off of school for summer break but were headed out the door to a day camp with the nanny when Mariah arrived.

"Your son and daughter look just like you and Dan," Mariah said as they relaxed under the shade of an umbrella. "They're really cute, and so polite."

They had been, too. Unlike so many kids that she'd met over the years, Adam and Alice had politely shook Mariah's hand. They seemed happy, calm, and well-behaved.

"When are you two going to have some kids?" Caroline

asked. "You'd both make great mothers."

Daphne vehemently shook her head. "Not me. I like other people's kids fine because you can give them back when they pee, poop, or cry, but I don't want any of my own. Too loud and messy. I'll stick with my two cats, thank you very much. I don't even scoop their litter. I bought one of those automatic litter boxes. All I have to do is change the bag every now and then. It's genius."

Now they were both looking at Mariah.

I guess it's my turn to share.

"I wouldn't mind having a child but it would have to be with the right man. I don't want to be one of those marriages where the father does nothing and the mother does everything. I'd want him to be involved."

Ryan would be an involved parent. He had strong opinions about how he was parented and none of them were very positive.

"Dan is a very hands-on father," Caroline said. "He was always better at getting the kids to sleep when they were babies. He could get a burp out of them when I'd failed."

"He sounds like a good dad," Daphne observed. "You both seem happy."

Caroline's smile dropped. "We are. I love him so much. I'm just afraid that I'm hurting him with all of this crying over Brad. I don't want him to think that I don't love him or our family."

"I'm sure he wouldn't think that," Mariah replied. "I'm sure he understands that it's just the past got dug up. No one was prepared for Brad to be found after all of these years."

Caroline was wringing her hands together, the knuckles white. "I'm realizing now that I haven't really dealt with all of my emotions from back then. I loved Brad, or I thought I did, and then he was gone suddenly. Just gone. No warning. Nothing prepares a person for that. So I made up a story in my head and tried to move on with my life. Apparently, I did a lousy job at it because look where I am now."

"I think you're handling it quite well," Daphne declared. "This was a shock to all of us and you wouldn't be human if you weren't upset. You and Theo were the closest to Brad, after all."

"Theo didn't seem upset yesterday," Caroline replied. "And I was all weepy."

"Men are taught not to express their emotions," Mariah reminded her friend. "Just because he didn't cry doesn't mean that he wasn't sad or upset."

The sound of Ted barking interrupted whatever Caroline had been about to say. The back door opened and Dan and Ryan walked out of the house and into the backyard, the beagle at their heels.

"Honey, Ryan is here to talk to us," Dan said taking a seat at the round table.

Ryan sat in the empty chair next to Mariah. Today he was wearing casual blue jeans and a light blue button-down shirt, the sleeves rolled up. He didn't look like a man on a mission, but she knew for a fact that he wasn't here to socialize. He'd told her last night that he was going to try and talk to everyone in their friend group today, if at all possible.

Ryan greeted them briefly, but basically got right down to business.

"I'm talking to everyone that was at the bar that night to try and get a better picture of the evening and what might have been going on in Brad's life. Yesterday, I spoke with Carl and this morning I talked to Theo."

Daphne checked her watch. "Wow, you were up early then. It's barely ten o'clock."

"I didn't want to waste any time." He shifted his focus to Caroline. "I also just spoke with Dan so I do need to ask you some questions. Can you talk to me about that night?"

Dan reached for Caroline's hand as she took a deep breath and straightened her shoulders as if bracing for a blow.

"I can. I want to help find out what happened to Brad."

"Great, then let's start at the beginning. Tell me about that night, even details that don't seem important. Take your time. There's no rush."

Caroline took another deep breath. "Brad wanted to go out and party, which as you know wasn't unusual. I was a little worried about getting up early to catch our flight but he said that it would be fine and that I could go home early if I wanted to. He never really needed all that much sleep so I didn't think it would be a big deal. We went to the bar and met Theo, who was already there. Everybody else started showing up. You and Mariah got there last. We'd already had a few cocktails and had been dancing. Well, I was dancing. Brad hated to dance."

"Was he in a good mood that night? Was anything bothering

him?"

Frowning, Caroline shook her head. "He was fine, just like always. I didn't notice anything out of the ordinary. He had been a little moody since he got home from school a few weeks before but he said he was just stressed out and he needed to have some fun."

Ryan didn't follow up right away, appearing to be struggling with his next question. After Mariah's conversation with him last night she had an inkling of what he wanted to ask but was afraid to.

Caroline and Dan exchanged a glance and then Dan nodded to his wife.

"It's okay, honey. We don't have anything to hide."

Returning her gaze to Ryan, Caroline smiled weakly. "I knew about Brad's other girls if that's what you were trying to ask me about. For the first few years that we dated, he tried to hide all of that from me but that last year...he didn't bother as much. Sometimes I think he wanted me to find out. He wanted us to argue, yell, and scream. Brad loved a good fight. He always said it cleared the air. He was always in a better mood after we'd argued. I, on the other hand, despised confrontation and avoided it until he pushed me into it. So yes, Ryan, I knew about Brad's extracurricular activities, and at that point I didn't care. I was planning to end things with Brad after Hawaii."

Mariah hadn't been expecting that declaration. Not at all.

Had Brad known? Did he care?

It was beginning to look like the past that Mariah had

known had never really actually existed.

What other surprises were there?

SO CAROLINE HAD known pretty much the whole time?

Ryan couldn't help but ask the next question. "You knew he was cheating but you stayed with him?"

The couple exchanged another glance and Dan patted his wife's hand in a comforting gesture.

"I'm not sure I can explain, but I'll try," Caroline said. "I was brought up to think that men would sow their wild oats when they were young and then later they would settle down. When I complained to my mom that Brad was cheating, she'd just tell me that he was young and he'd eventually stop. I really believed that. I truly thought that he would stop running after other girls, but eventually I got tired of waiting. I could clearly see that other couples didn't have the same problems. You never ran around on Mariah, and it was obvious you loved her. I wanted someone to love and respect me like that. So I'd decided to break up with Brad after the Hawaii trip. I didn't want to ruin everyone's vacation, and it didn't seem to matter if I waited a few weeks. I'd already waited far too long anyway."

Caroline's mother sounded like a 1950s nightmare of a parent. She'd actively encouraged her daughter to stay with a boy that disrespected her.

And Ryan hadn't ever cheated on Mariah. He'd never wanted to, and she would have dumped his ass if he had. Even back then she'd been a force to be reckoned with. She certainly hadn't put up with much shit.

"Did Brad know that you knew?"

A few tears slid down Caroline's cheeks. "Of course, he did. He liked to pretend that I was just *confused* or that I didn't *understand*. He would never admit it out loud."

"Did he know you were going to break up with him?"

"I don't know," she confessed. "I don't think so, although I gave him plenty of warning. I kept telling him that eventually I wasn't going to put up with his bad behavior anymore."

But if she never actually broke up with him, Brad might have thought that she never would. She'd put up with him forever.

"Had you...already moved on?"

Shit, he didn't know quite how to word this, especially in front of Danny.

"If you're talking about Trent, I know about all of that," Danny said with a smug smile. "We don't have any secrets from each other. Trent was a long time ago and frankly, he doesn't matter anymore."

"Not that he ever mattered," Caroline said firmly. "I was only trying to show Brad that he wasn't the only person that could cheat. I could, too."

"So Brad knew about you and Trent?" Ryan asked. "Did you tell him?"

Caroline shook her head. "No, I never did. I was going to because I wanted to hurt him and then I realized that he wasn't worth it. I'd already decided to end things."

"So you and Trent…"

"Had a fling," Caroline replied with a shrug. "It was short and forgettable, to be honest. It meant nothing. It was just petty revenge on my part and I'm not very proud of that."

"You are absolutely sure that Brad didn't know? Could Trent have told him?"

"If Trent told Brad that he and Caroline were sleeping together, we all would have known about it," Danny said. "Brad and Trent would have definitely argued or possibly even physically fought."

That was exactly what Ryan was thinking as well. Had Brad and Trent argued that night so long ago?

One thing was for sure…one of them had ended up dead.

CHAPTER FIFTEEN

TRENT GARFIELD HAD done well for himself in the last decade. A quick search into his background had turned up a man who made a great deal of money and liked to spend it. Trent had a bevy of women and an active social life. When he wasn't squiring a date to a charity winetasting or a fundraising gala, he was playing golf with his friends or jetting off for a ski weekend in Aspen.

He'd joined his family's real estate business and worked out of his home which was where Ryan caught up with him later in the afternoon after visiting Caroline and Danny. Trent lived in a penthouse apartment that overlooked Lake Michigan. Decorated in chrome and white, it really wasn't Ryan's taste, but he had to admit that no one would be looking at the furniture with a view like that.

"Can I get you a drink?" Trent said, ushering Ryan into the living room. The drapes were all pulled open to reveal wall to ceiling windows. "I've got just about anything you could want. Soda, water, beer, or something harder if the mood takes you."

"Thank you, but I'm good." Ryan settled on the couch.

"You know why I'm here so I guess we should just get down to it. I'm talking to everyone about the night that Brad disappeared. What they remember. That sort of thing."

Trent sat down, his body sprawled and a water bottle dangling from his fingers. Today, he was dressed in jeans and a t-shirt that made him look like a college kid again. When Ryan had made the appointment with him, he'd said it was the perfect day because he didn't have any outside meetings.

"I don't remember much," Trent admitted. "I was hammered that night. I'm not sure how much I can help you."

"Did you talk to Brad? What did he say?"

Trent shook his head. "I don't think that we had any sort of conversation beyond whose turn it was to go to the bar and get the drinks. He was hanging around with Theo and Caro, and I'd met some girl, too. Can't remember her name but we danced and had some drinks. That's pretty much it. I didn't see much of him that night, to be honest, and I didn't stay late. We all had to catch a plane the next day."

"Were you surprised that Brad didn't make the flight?"

Smiling, Trent rubbed at his chin. "Shit, you know how he was as well as I do. He sort of marched to his own drummer, if you know what I mean. He didn't like rules and he loved causing chaos. So...no, I wasn't surprised at all. I will say that I was surprised that he never showed up. I thought he'd fly in the next day and make a big entrance. He liked to be the center of attention."

That was the pot calling the kettle...

"So do you."

"Can't deny it," Trent said with a cocky grin. "I was born to make a splash. It was my destiny."

He doesn't have a self-esteem issue. But then he never did.

"You two argued a few days before. What was it about?"

Trent's grin vanished and his body language went from relaxed to tense in less than three seconds. He was now sitting straight up, his lips a thin line.

"Who told you that?"

"Everyone knew. What was it about?"

"It wasn't a big deal. We were a couple of idiots that argued about stupid shit, that's all."

"Since it was so stupid, you won't mind telling me what it was then."

Shoulders stiffening, Trent stood from the chair. "The fact is I don't really remember all the details. It was dumb stuff."

"Was it about Caroline?"

Trent turned his back on Ryan, staring out of the large windows. "Why would we argue about her?"

"Because you and Caroline were sleeping together. You don't have to pretend. I talked to Caroline this morning and she admitted it, plus she was seen going into your room in Hawaii."

Turning around, Trent shrugged carelessly. "It wasn't about Caroline. Frankly, she was never important enough to argue about. I wasn't in love with her or anything, and she sure as hell wasn't in love with me. She just wanted to get back at Brad and I was convenient."

"So Brad didn't know?"

"Not that I know of. Unless she told him, of course."

Ryan wasn't sure he was buying what Trent was selling.

"You're telling me that you were sleeping with Brad's girl-friend and you didn't tell him? I find that hard to believe. I think you would have loved to tell him."

"I would have," Trent smirked. "But I never got the chance. I was going to tell him when we were all in Hawaii."

"Why didn't you tell him that night?"

"Because he was drunk and so was I. I wanted him as close to sober as I could get when I told him."

Hell of a weird friendship.

"You hated him that much?"

"I didn't hate Brad at all," Trent laughed with a shake of his head. "Brad was just...Brad. We'd grown up together. Let's face it, Ryan, we never got a chance to decide if we liked or didn't like each other. From the time we could walk we were all shoved in a group and told to be friends because our parents liked to hang out together. Did I like Brad? Hell if I know. Did you? Do you even really know how you felt about him? He didn't make it easy to like him, now did he?"

Ryan didn't like to think – or speak – ill of the dead. His parents had drilled that into his head.

"Brad had some issues..."

Trent's brows shot up. "Issues? That's a fucking understatement. He was a mess, and I'll be honest here with you that I'm not surprised he ended up with his skull bashed in. He was a loudmouthed asshole who spent most of his time drunk and belligerent, but thought he was the coolest dude that ever lived. Yeah, he was cool when we were seventeen, but by the time we were twenty-one his antics were getting a little old. At least for me. Your mileage may vary, but I think you had less patience for his shit than I did. You just covered it better."

"It's sounds like you hate him."

"I'll say this again – I didn't hate him. I didn't love him either. He could be fun, I'll admit that. I liked competing with him because he was so easy to provoke. He hated to fucking lose at anything, and he was a sore winner, too. I was looking forward to Caroline screaming my name when he fucked her."

It was hard for Ryan to believe he'd once been friends with these people, but he had. It didn't say much for his own taste.

I was young and didn't know shit.

"Do you hear yourself talking?" Ryan asked, exasperation in his tone. "You sound like the asshole here, not Brad."

"I'm just telling it like it is. You wanted honesty and now you've got it. You just don't like what I'm saying, but you know that I'm right about Brad. That's why you two weren't close that last year. I heard he tried something with Mariah, but I don't think that's true."

So the friend group had been talking about that? Ryan shouldn't have been surprised. They talked about everyone.

"You think Brad was garbage but you don't think he tried something with Mariah? That doesn't make sense."

Trent's smile grew wider. "I think that because if Brad had tried anything with Mariah you would have broken both of his arms and his pretty face, too."

Ryan hadn't broken any of Brad's bones but he'd wanted to. It had only been the pleadings of Mariah that had kept him from doing it. She hadn't wanted what happened to ripple through their friend group.

"I have more self-control than that."

"Not about Mariah, you don't. I was always surprised that you two didn't get married."

Lots of people had been surprised.

"Some things aren't meant to be."

"I don't believe in love," Trent declared. "At least not for me, but I always thought that if anyone had that it was you and Mariah."

At one point, I thought that, too.

"Love isn't always enough." Ryan didn't want to discuss his relationships. He needed to steer the conversation back on track. "I have one more question. Where did you go when you left the bar that night?"

"I went back to my place. Caroline showed up about thirty minutes later and stayed until about five."

That didn't match earlier statements.

"Caroline told me that she went home alone."

"She may have left the bar alone but she didn't stay that way. She showed up at my door half-drunk."

"Her story is that she went straight home, went to sleep, and then to the airport in the morning."

"I'm not lying. I was with her."

"Can you prove it?"

Laughing, Trent shook his head. "No, but then neither can she."

That was true. That was the problem with cold cases.

"Wait," Trent said, holding up his hand. "There might be someone that can back up my story. The guy who lived across the hall from me was a real night owl. If I came home from the bar alone, he would sometimes come over and we'd drink a few beers."

"How did he know if you were alone?"

"His balcony window overlooked my parking space. He'd sit out there and smoke. He might remember Caroline showing up that night."

"I'll check him out. What was his name?"

"Steve Alton. I remember that he had a weekly sports column in one of those newspapers that they give out free."

That information narrowed it down just enough that Ryan might actually find the guy. But would he remember a random night over ten years ago?

"I'll try and find him. Talk to him."

"Tell him I said hello." Trent settled back down into the chair, his confidence returned. "I'm telling you the truth. I don't have anything to hide. I didn't like Brad that much but I didn't hurt him. I didn't have any reason to."

It appeared that no one had a reason to, but somehow Brad had ended up dead. And Ryan didn't think that it was an accident.

CHAPTER SIXTEEN

G RANT HILLARD WAS a great guy. He owned his own successful business. He was intelligent, funny, and knew how to pair wines with food. He was well-read, well-traveled, and not in the least pretentious. Mariah had been on three dates with him and had enjoyed herself each time.

But…something was missing. There was no spark, no excitement. Her pulse didn't pound and she didn't get breathless when she saw him even though he was quite good-looking. Today they were having lunch together because he needed to fly out on the red-eye for a business meeting in San Francisco.

"I was thinking about getting us tickets to a show for next week," Grant said, digging into his salmon. "What do you think?"

What did she think? She didn't know.

To be honest, she'd barely paid attention the last twenty minutes or so.

I was thinking about Ryan. Dammit.

"A show? That sounds like fun."

Setting his fork on the side of his plate, Grant dabbed at the corners of his mouth with a napkin. "Your expression doesn't match your words."

"How so?"

"Your words said it sounded like fun but your face looked like I was inviting you to a root canal with no anesthesia."

Luckily, Grant was smiling so he wasn't upset.

"I...don't know why my face was doing that," Mariah admitted with a sigh. "I haven't had a great couple of days, to be honest."

"Is there anything I can do to help?"

He was a nice guy. Really nice. She should be really attracted to him but...she wasn't. There was no zing.

I want the zing. I admit it.

"It's sweet that you offered but I think this is something I'm going to have to work out for myself. I'm just not the most patient person and I want it all to be fine right away."

He nodded in understanding. "I get that. I can be impatient as well."

"You seem pretty calm and relaxed," Mariah observed.

"I try but everyone has their moments." He leaned forward, his elbows resting on the table between them. "You can talk to me if you want. I'm a good listener."

Did Mariah even want to talk about it? And with Grant? One of the main rules of dating was that you didn't talk about an old boyfriend with a new one.

"I guess I'm still upset about my friend Brad," she finally replied, taking a more neutral path. "It's all been such a shock."

She'd mentioned the situation to Grant so he knew some but not all the details.

"You and Brad were close?"

"We were all part of the same friend group, but no, we weren't best friends. But we all hung out together throughout our youth."

"Then it must have been hard when he disappeared."

"It was the not knowing that I think was the worst. Everyone had their own way of dealing with it. Some of us sort of made up stories in our heads about what might have happened. Apparently, Brad used to joke about faking his own death and running a tiki bar on some tropical island."

"Faking one's own death is probably harder in real life than it is on television or in the movies," Grant said with a smile.

"I know," Mariah conceded. "But none of us wanted to really admit that he might be dead. Now we can't be in denial anymore."

"What did happen to Brad? Was it an accident?"

"Probably not, although we don't know what really happened that night. Ryan is here investigating for the family. He's one of our friend group that became a cop. He's talking to everyone about that night and trying to put together what might have really happened."

Grant reached for his water glass. "Ryan? That's your ex-boyfriend, isn't it?"

How on earth…? Liza. It had to be. She'd fixed them up.

"Yes, although I'm left wondering how you knew that."

"When Liza gave me the rundown about you, she said that you'd had two major relationships in your life – your marriage and Ryan Beck. You were with him a long time."

"That's true."

"Was it an amicable split?"

"Yes, there was no histrionics, no screaming or yelling. We both agreed it was for the best."

"So seeing him again isn't strange?"

It was strange. Very strange. And disturbing. She hadn't slept well last night and it was all Ryan's fault.

I wonder if he still has insomnia. He never slept well.

"I saw him at Liza's wedding," she said, dodging the question. "We have friends in common so it's not like I haven't seen him in the last decade."

His gaze was intent as if he could see far too much truth. Did it show that Ryan could still make her crazy?

"We decided to be friends," she continued, her words rushed. "And it's for the best. That way Liza won't feel so weird when we're all together. We were friends before we dated and now we're friends again. It's working fine."

"Mariah, you are a terrible liar. Just horrendous. Don't take up poker for a living."

Crap, it did show. This wasn't good news. Could Ryan see it, too?

Sighing, she took a gulp of her iced tea. "Am I that bad?"

"Maybe not to the average person, but remember I am a professional. I'm a jury consultant, Mariah. It's my business to see what people want to hide from others. Body language is more than a hobby for me."

"He'll be gone soon. He never stays in Chicago very long."

"And how do you feel about that?"

"I–I'm okay with it. Like I said, we're friends. That's it."

Grant's gaze dropped to his hands and then back up to her. "I think...that just maybe...this guy affects you more than you want to admit. I think you still have feelings for him."

She shook her head, denying his words. "No, I don't. It's been over for many years."

"You know, it's really okay," Grant replied with a grimace. "I like you, Mariah. You're beautiful, funny, smart, and talented. You're exactly like the person that I've been hoping to find."

There was a *but* at the end of that sentence.

"But?" she prompted.

"I kind of get the feeling that you're not into me."

It appeared that he could read her like a book. She wasn't sure she was a fan of that.

"I like you a lot. You're a great guy. Really terrific."

"There was definitely a *but* at the end of that sentence," he said with a grin. "But I just don't do it for you, right? It's okay, Mariah. I promise I won't get all weepy and start writing bad poetry."

He didn't seem the type, honestly. Her ego should be a tad more bruised but it actually kind of helped that he wasn't heartbroken. She didn't want to hurt anyone.

"I'm a terrible person," she stated firmly. "I should be head over heels for a guy like you. You're great."

"You are not a terrible person," Grant laughed. "Not even close. It's just not happening for us and that's okay. I'll tell you what…how about you and I be friends and you and your ex-boyfriend rekindle your romance? I think you still have some feelings there."

"I do," she admitted and not happily. "But I don't want to have feelings for him. There were good reasons we split up when we did. We were both so young and we hadn't experienced anything of life. Plus, Ryan is so damn stubborn. Do you know he never admitted he was wrong? Ever. Well, until yesterday. He admitted it then and apologized but that's how stubborn he could be. He didn't want to compromise on anything."

"It sounds like he does now. Do you think he might have changed?"

Ryan had changed. The question was…how much?

"I do, but it's been a long time. I'm not sure we even know each other anymore."

"Then get to know each other," Grant suggested. "It sounds like you still care about him. It might be worth finding out if he feels the same. But let me suggest that you might know more about him than you think you do. You spent your formative years together, after all. Sure, he might be stubborn but is he a good person? Is he honest? Hardworking? Does he care about others and have empathy? Do your morals and values align?"

"He's all of those things."

And more.

"Do you think he still has feelings for you?"

"That's a loaded question," Mariah said, pleating the napkin between her nervous fingers. It was a query that she hadn't wanted to think about too closely, afraid of the answer. "I have no idea how he feels. I know that his original plan was to avoid me."

That statement made Grant smile.

"Then he still feels something. If he didn't, then it wouldn't be any big deal to be around you. It sounds like you and this Ryan have some unfinished business."

Mariah frowned. "Is this what you usually do on dates? Talk the women into going after other men? It seems like a rather limiting strategy."

"I'm an idiot when it comes to love and relationships. But there is one thing I know for sure, and it's that I want the person I'm dating to be totally into me. If not, then I need to move along. No harm, no foul. No recriminations. Maybe friends were all we were meant to be."

"You want to be friends with me?"

"Everyone can use more friends."

It was almost the exact same thing she'd said to Ryan.

"I think that I'd like to have you for a friend. You're a nice person, and wise, too."

"I like laying some wisdom down every now and then. So what are you going to do about Ryan?"

"I have no idea," she confessed with an uncomfortable laugh. "I'm not sure that I'm convinced that he's still carrying a torch.

He doesn't seem the type."

"Keep your eyes open when you're with him. I can give you some body language advice if you'd like it."

Mariah wasn't sure she wanted it. She wasn't sure she wanted to do anything about Ryan. Or their relationship.

Because if Ryan still had feelings...and she had feelings...then what in the hell were they going to do about it? She didn't want to go after something that was destined to fall apart anyway.

Was Ryan best left in the past? Or did they deserve a second chance?

She didn't have any answers, but one thing was certain. She didn't want a second heartbreak at the hands of Ryan Beck. She'd barely survived the first one.

CHAPTER SEVENTEEN

AFTER FINISHING UP with Trent, Ryan headed back to his apartment. He'd received a message from the office that they had information for him, and he wanted a chance to sit down where it was quiet and review it all. He only had Isla left to talk to and she was being difficult, being vague about when they could meet. Stepping out of his cab in front of his building, he was greeted with a sight that he didn't like at all. A rush of emotion punched at his gut, almost taking his breath away.

Mariah. And another man. Hugging on the sidewalk. She looked happy.

Why am I so angry that she's happy? I should want her to be happy.

And I'm not angry. I'm just surprised.

Happy, but not *that* happy.

This – feeling – wasn't welcome. He didn't have any business being jealous of Mariah in the arms of a man. He didn't want to be jealous either. It wasn't convenient in the least. He was still working on trying to be friends with her, and now he wanted to knock that guy into the street and let a bus run over him.

He must have been standing there staring because eventually she noticed him, giving him a cheery wave as she bid the man goodbye. She stood on the sidewalk as he drove away before turning back to Ryan, who still hadn't been able to move from his spot.

Just like that. In a mere split second more than a decade had melted away and he was twenty-two again. Life hadn't seemed nearly as difficult or complex. Twelve years ago he would have strode up to Mariah and pulled her into his arms, kissing her senseless.

Today? He wasn't going to do that. He was going to remember that they weren't a couple anymore. That he'd moved on.

Funny, I don't feel like I've moved on, though. Is this why I didn't want to see her?

It was like being hit on the head with a clue-by-four. He'd wanted to avoid Mariah because his emotions when it came to her were messy. They'd separated mutually back then but he'd never found anyone that made him feel the way she had.

And it appeared that she still could. Shit, this was not good. Clearly, she'd moved on. Married, divorced, and now dating someone. She wasn't losing any goddamn sleep over him.

Now he was even more pissed off.

"Who was that?"

Christ on a cracker, could he be any more obvious about his jealousy? He needed to keep his mouth shut but for some reason that was proving more difficult than usual.

"A friend of mine. We had lunch."

He held the door open for her and they entered the much cooler lobby.

"A friend? Or a boyfriend?"

He wanted to slam his head into the wall but instead he simply pushed the button to call the elevator.

I am such an idiot.

Mariah didn't appear perturbed about his intrusive questions, which only served to piss him off more.

"It was a date. If that's what you're asking."

"I wasn't asking anything."

"It sounded like you were asking if he was my boyfriend."

"Why would I ask that?"

The doors slid open and they stepped into the elevator. Ryan tugged at his collar, wishing he were just about anywhere but here.

"I don't know. How about we change the subject? What time are we leaving for dinner?"

Ryan had completely forgotten that they were supposed to go to dinner with his parents that night. Together. Like they were a couple.

"You don't have to go."

Shit, that sounded rude. He hadn't meant it to come out like that. He'd just wanted to give her an out. His parents had put her on the spot yesterday.

"Why would I not go? I told your parents that I'd be there."

"They didn't really let you say no."

"If I had wanted to say no, I would have said no. But I want to go. I like your parents and I love the cook's roast chicken."

"It's just chicken."

The doors slid open and they stepped into the hallway, the tension thick between them. He followed her to her apartment door.

"Ryan, can you please just say what you mean?" she asked, placing her key in the lock. "Did you want to have dinner with your parents alone? Because if you do, then I'll stay home."

That sounded like one of Dante's circles of hell. A four-course dinner of torture.

"No, but–"

"Then I'm going. If you don't want to ride together, I can go on my own. Just let me know."

"Fine, and you don't have to be so snippy about it. I was just giving you a chance to bow out if you really didn't want to go. I would think you'd be more grateful."

Even their arguing felt familiar, but not nearly as catastrophic as it had seemed when they were younger. Then every disagreement had been bigger and more important than it really was. Now, this was only some light bickering.

Her brows shot up. "Did you just call me snippy, Ryan Beck? You better take that back quick."

"I take it back," he said immediately, holding up his hands in surrender. He'd only said it to get a reaction from her. It was a bad habit from the past. "I'm sorry."

"Snippy," she muttered under her breath. "Really? I should

make you go to your parents' dinner all by yourself for that crack, buster."

"I really am sorry," he apologized again. "I don't know why I'm trying to pick a fight with you."

She stepped into the apartment and tossed her purse on the kitchen counter. "I know why you're doing it. You're doing it to keep me at arm's length. Mission accomplished. I don't want to be around you right now. Congratulations."

He opened his mouth to tell her she was wrong but then snapped it shut again. She was probably right. If they were arguing, then he wouldn't think about how much he'd missed her all these years. How he still thought about her when it was most inconvenient.

Like when he was with other women.

If he was completely honest with himself, he'd been comparing his dates with Mariah his entire adult life. He didn't enjoy the feeling that he'd been that disingenuous in his relationships. It didn't speak well of him and the women deserved better.

"I appreciate the apology," she said, holding the door open for him. "Now I think I'd like to lie down and rest for a little while. You can send me a text and let me know what time we're leaving for dinner."

She was mad at him. Hell, he was mad at himself. It might be a good idea to give them both some space.

"We can leave at six if that's convenient."

"It's fine."

Apparently, Ryan didn't know shit about women, but one

thing he did know was that it wasn't a good thing when they said something was *fine*. It wasn't *fine*, and he was going to hear about it at some point.

"I'll call you later."

"Fine."

Shit...two *fines* in a row. He was in the doghouse and eating Milk-Bones.

Since the minute his plane had touched down in Chicago, he'd been acting like an asshole to Mariah. It had to stop.

Something had to change. Because one very important thing hadn't.

He still had feelings for Mariah Campbell.

MARIAH WAS STILL fuming when she slammed her door shut the minute that Ryan exited her apartment. Yes, it was petty, but that was the mood she was in at the moment. He was being a jerk on purpose and she was tired of it. They'd been circling each other like two boxers and she was exhausted. They weren't getting anywhere – which she assumed was the whole point of his behavior – and she couldn't take much more.

Grant had hit a nerve at lunch when he'd pointed out that she and Ryan had unfinished business. Mariah had managed to dig a hole and bury it but since his arrival it had brought up so much emotion from the past.

I'm not completely over him. I still miss him.

They'd had their issues but looking back they didn't seem so insurmountable now. When she was young, she'd thought that they needed to agree on everything. Now she could see that was a naive hope. She didn't want to date a carbon copy of herself. She wanted to be challenged and shown new things.

He hadn't been much better, though. He'd been so stubborn when at least she'd been open to compromise. Except her idea of compromise was that he needed to be more like her. His idea of compromise was that everything went his way. It was a recipe for disaster. But then, they'd been so young. They hadn't known shit about life or relationships.

When it all came down to it, Ryan Beck was still the best man she'd ever known. Bar none. Frankly, it wasn't even a close race.

So now what?

She didn't have a clue. She only knew that she and Ryan had history and that neither one of them was very good at ignoring it.

BACK AT HIS own apartment, Ryan made himself a sandwich and popped open a soda before settling at the kitchen island to eat. As much as his brain wanted to dwell on the problem across the hall, he needed to lasso his thoughts and stay on track. He was in Chicago to figure out what happened to Brad. That had to be his priority. His personal problems were lower down the list. Halfway through his turkey on rye, he called his boss Jared Monroe.

"How's Chicago?"

Jared must have been working from home because there was the definite sound of laughing children in the background. He and his wife had two, plus a dog named after Stevie Nicks, the singer from Fleetwood Mac.

"Hot, but that's not unusual in the summer."

"Have some Chicago pizza for me. Man, I love that stuff."

"I haven't yet but I will. I got your message. What have you got for me? I can't believe you were able to find anything on Brad's finances. It was over ten years ago. That's amazing."

"It wasn't that difficult, actually," Jared chuckled. "Your friend's finances were all wound up in his family's finances, and most of those accounts are still around. Plus nothing is ever really deleted in this world of computer databases. You might have to dig a little bit, but eventually you'll find it."

Jared was known for finding out information that others couldn't get. Ryan didn't know what witchcraft or voodoo the older man used, but it came in damn useful at times.

"So I'll just get right to the important question. Did you find anything interesting?"

"Depends on what you call interesting and what you may already know about Bradley Harrington. He spent a hell of a lot of money, and his family didn't seem to mind. They kept him supplied with cash and a pretty much unlimited credit line which he used with abandon. Clothes, trips, booze, and what looks like gifts to females. Perfume, lingerie, jewelry. That sort of stuff."

"I know all of that," Ryan admitted. "Brad loved to be the guy that picked up the tab or bought several rounds. For all his issues, he was generous as hell. I heard that he paid a bunch of bills for a classmate in college because that guy didn't have any family to help him and was working two jobs plus school."

"He sounds like a decent guy, but that's not all I found out."

"I'm listening."

Maybe Jared had found something that would help the investigation. Right now, Ryan didn't feel like he'd made any progress at all.

"Your friend was a gambler. Big time. Did you know that?"

"I knew he gambled," Ryan replied carefully. "When you say he was a big gambler, how big are you talking about? Like he bet a lot of money on the Super Bowl? Because, Brad did like to make bets on football."

"He spent a hell of a lot of money on it year-round so I suspect that he bet on more than football. It looks like he gambled regularly."

Brad was addicted to gambling? It wasn't the most far-fetched thing that Ryan could find out about his old friend. When Brad loved something, he loved it a lot. More than anything. When he did anything, he went all out, balls to the wall. There were never any half-measures. It was go big or go home.

"How did you find this? I can't imagine that he put his gambling on his credit card."

"He didn't, but he did make regular withdrawals and sometimes transferred money to other accounts. I also followed his cell phone records and they led to about half a dozen bookies in Chicago and New York City. Looks like he was spreading his bets around so he could bet the maximum amount each day. And from what I can see, he did bet every single day."

"I had no idea he was that bad," Ryan finally replied, his brain running through so many images from the past. "I know that he liked to place a few bets on sports, but I don't think any of us knew the extent of his problem. I thought it was a few innocent bets. I placed a couple myself on the playoffs or the big game. I didn't think it was a big deal."

"From what I can find, your friend was betting up to seventy-five thousand dollars a day. That's just an estimate, though. I could be wrong. It might be more or less, but I think it's a decent guess."

A *day*? That was insane.

"His family didn't know? I can't imagine that he was in so deep without them knowing he was spending money like that."

"I can't answer that question. Maybe his family only looked at monthly totals, for example. Then they'd see that he spent more than he won but they wouldn't see all the details for each day. Or maybe they didn't monitor his spending at all. There's also a chance they knew and didn't care. Do the parents gamble? I'm wondering if the son learned from mom or dad."

"I don't know but it looks like I'm going to need to ask that question."

It was going to be awkward as hell too, depending on Skip

and Lilly's attitude regarding gambling. Ryan was almost positive that Skip bet on golf when he played with Ryan's dad.

"Did you get anything else from his phone activity?"

"Names of a few women you may not have talked to yet. He had an active social life, that's for sure. Parties, bars, restaurants, nightclubs. All of that and more. He did slow down a little during his last semester, but the gambling stayed the same. If anything, it intensified."

Ryan would need to talk to Caroline again and see if she knew anything about the gambling. Theo, too. If anyone knew it would be Brad's best friend.

I have a feeling that perhaps a few people haven't been completely candid with me. And what about Isla? Did she know?

"Can you text me the information for the women? I'll make arrangements for Rosenthal to talk to them."

"Will do. How are your interviews going? Anything to report?"

"Not really. Everyone says that Brad was acting normally that night and in the weeks before. They all thought that he'd show up in Hawaii and were surprised that he didn't." A thought occurred to Ryan. "I know this is going to sound insane but they kept bringing up how Brad would talk about faking his own death. I don't suppose you could check on that? Maybe find out if he looked into buying a one-way ticket to Fiji? Can you even get information like that from the distant past?"

"If it's in a computer database somewhere we can try," Jared replied, confidence in his tone. "Listen, I don't mean to be an asshole here, but your friend talked about faking his own death? Why? Did he hate his life or something? Were his parents abusive to him?"

"Not that I know of but Brad liked to be different, quirky. He thought it was cool to be rich and eccentric. He thought the idea of running away from society and living barefoot on the beach was kind of romantic."

"He sounds like an interesting guy," Jared remarked. "Definitely not boring."

"That's true. He was never dull. He always had something going on."

Did Brad have something going on that had gotten him killed? Ryan was beginning to think the answer might be yes. Time to backtrack to the parents and Theo. He had new questions to ask.

CHAPTER EIGHTEEN

S O FAR, DINNER hadn't been the ordeal that Mariah had expected it to be. Ryan had been friendly and polite to his parents, and Jack and Patricia hadn't made any digs about being a cop or not joining the family business. All in all, it had been quite pleasant.

Of course, Mariah wasn't in the same boat as Ryan. She actually liked his mom and dad. They seemed like good people who loved their children, but perhaps didn't always know how to show that emotion. Instead they bought them things hoping their American Express card would do the talking.

How Ryan couldn't see this, Mariah didn't know. He was one of the most intelligent men she'd ever known but when it came to his family he couldn't see past the end of his nose. He was just angry that they weren't the kind of parents that he'd wanted so he'd set out to be the son they didn't want either. No one wanted to budge from their position which made the entire situation more frustrating for everyone around them.

Liza had been working on her parents for years, telling them to back off Ryan about his career choices. She'd also been working on Ryan, and Mariah had been as well when they'd still been together. She hadn't made much progress though, and he'd constantly tried to avoid spending any time with them. Deep inside, she felt that he'd regret that eventually. His parents weren't going to live forever, after all.

"So how is the investigation going, son?" Jack asked as the dinner plates were whisked away. "Any progress?"

They'd somehow managed to avoid talking about Brad during the meal, instead discussing the upcoming party for Patricia's birthday which had led to an even more in-depth debate about the merits of the Caribbean versus Europe. Jack was planning to take his wife on an extended vacation as part of her birthday present and they were trying to decide where to go. They'd already traveled extensively so neither location would be new to them. Mariah had suggested an Alaskan cruise as her parents had just returned from one and were still raving about it.

Ryan dabbed at the corners of his mouth with the heavy linen napkin. "I'm still putting together a picture of what happened that night when we were all together. I still have to speak to a few people including Isla Norton. She's had a busy schedule but I'm hoping that I get to talk to her tomorrow. My boss has also done some research into Brad's finances and came up with a few leads for me to follow."

This was the first that Mariah was hearing about new leads. She'd specifically asked Ryan in the car on the way there how his day had gone. He'd said it was fine but he hadn't elaborated on it any further so she'd assumed that meant there was nothing to talk about. Apparently, she'd been wrong.

Liza's brows rose expectantly. "You can't just throw something out there like that and then clam up, big brother. Talk. What did your boss find out? Was Brad funding an underground research facility that was trying to weaponize trained sharks?"

Her husband Mike grinned. "Or even better, a clandestine paramilitary group that goes around and helps people in trouble like 'The A-Team'?"

Chuckling, Jack smiled. "I think both of you watch too much television. I doubt it was anything very interesting. What would Ryan find if he looked into your finances, I wonder?"

"That I like shoes," Liza sighed. "And Italian takeout. He'd find out that Mike plays too much golf."

"There's no such thing," Mike said with a mock anger tone in his voice. "Golf is a great way to spend a lazy Saturday afternoon."

"Lying in a hammock drinking a lemonade is even better," Liza teased her husband, placing her hand on his. "Or you could spend time with your wife. Now there's a radical idea."

"I'm just giving you time to go shopping," Mike replied with a grin. "We both have our little hobbies."

"So…what were Brad's hobbies?" Liza asked, taking a sip from her water goblet. "We know he played golf and partied."

For a moment, Mariah didn't think that Ryan was going to respond but he did, although she could tell it was a reluctant reply.

"I haven't had a chance to talk to Skip and Lilly about this so

I would appreciate your discretion until I do. It's all going to come out eventually I would imagine, but I'd like them to hear it directly from me since I'm the one working on the case."

"That's fine, Ryan," Patricia murmured. "We're not gossips."

"I didn't think that you were," he assured his mother. "I just need you all to know that this is not common knowledge. Brad appeared to be gambling quite a bit. Every single day, as a matter of fact. He may have had a gambling problem."

Those words were a punch in the chest to Mariah. If Brad had been gambling, did he owe people money? Had one of them hurt him that night?

"Do you know for sure?" Jack asked, his expression somber. "How did you even find something like this out? It was over ten years ago."

"His cell phone was on his dad's account, which still exists," Ryan explained. "They traced his calls to several bookies in major metropolitan areas. He would make multiple calls a day, plus he was taking regular withdrawals and also transferring money. I'm going to need to ask Skip and Lilly if they knew about it."

"I can guarantee you that Skip didn't know his son was gambling with multiple bookies," Jack said. "He never would have allowed that."

"I still have to ask him."

Ryan sounded defensive and immediately the tension in the room zoomed higher.

This could go so badly.

"I'm just saying that there's no way he would have known."

Straightening in his chair, Ryan lifted his chin defiantly. "And I'm just saying that I have to ask him. It's literally my job."

Jack sighed and shook his head. "What kind of a job has you asking good people nosy and intrusive questions? They've lost their son and you're going to make it worse."

That tension had spiked to the point where there was almost a physical wall that Mariah could actually see between Ryan and his father. It had been going so well…

"The kind of job that puts the bad people behind bars," Ryan said, his tone hard. He was frowning, his lips a thin, unhappy line. "And that means that even good people have to be asked uncomfortable questions. How much did they know about Brad's life? I don't know the answer to that and to be honest, neither do you. If Brad was a gambling addict do you honestly believe Skip would have told you? There's no way that would have happened because appearances are all that matters to you guys."

"That's not true," Patricia said. "We just care about Skip and Lilly. We don't want them hurt."

"I don't want to hurt them either, but do you know what would be worse? To have a killer go free because I was too much of a wimp to ask a few questions. If Skip and Lilly really want to find out what happened to their son, they're going to have to deal with finding out some facts that they may not like. Now, if all they want is to keep up the happy and loving family façade, I can pack my suitcase and be on the red-eye back home tonight."

Mariah reached out to place her hand on his arm. She could feel the tension in the muscles under her fingers. "Ryan, calm down. I'm sure your father–"

"Right," he interrupted, his tone derisive. "He didn't mean anything by it. Of course, he meant it. He hates my job and he always has. He doesn't approve. End of story."

"We don't hate your job," Lilly said. "I guess we just don't understand it."

Jack shrugged, his own face a match to his son's. Neither was happy. "We've never said we didn't like your job, but it's true that we'd rather you did something else. Your mother was constantly worried that you were going to be hurt or shot when you were a police officer. Being in law enforcement is dangerous and you never thought about how your decisions affected everyone else."

Ryan threw his linen napkin on the table. "You mean that if I'd just done what you told me to, then everyone would be happy. That's everyone but me, Dad. I wouldn't be happy. I'm doing what I love and I'm trying to help one of your best friends. It's still not good enough for you. If I'm not doing what you want, you're disappointed in me. And now tonight you're even trying to tell me how to be a damn cop."

"I'm not telling you how to do your job, I'm just telling you that Skip wouldn't have known if Brad had a gambling problem. If he had, he would have gotten him some help."

Liza and Mike hadn't said much in the last few minutes and Mariah didn't blame them. When Ryan and Jack went down this road, it was best to let them do it alone. Even Patricia appeared to be done with the conversation. She looked like she had so much to say, but it was clear she wasn't going to say anything at all.

"I'll just repeat myself that I still have to ask him," Ryan ground out. "My job isn't to make everyone feel good about themselves. Sometimes I have to ask the hard questions that make people uncomfortable. Sometimes I have to be the son of a bitch that tells a wife that her husband has been cheating on her and now he's a suspect in his girlfriend's murder. That's just the way it is. The truth doesn't care about our delicate feelings. It's just the truth."

Jack cleared his throat. "All I'm asking you to do is be kind when you talk to them. That's it."

"But you didn't ask, Dad," Ryan argued. "You never asked me to do that, and I would have done that anyway. I don't want to hurt them. But no, you never asked. If you had, I would have said yes."

"Fine," Jack huffed. "Ryan, will you please be kind to Skip and Lilly when you talk to them? They're going through hell and I don't want anyone making it any worse for them."

"The last thing I want to do is make it worse. Of course I will be kind. But I will do my job."

Everyone was quiet at the table. The tension still thick. No one seemed to want to speak and that made Mariah antsy. She couldn't take the prolonged silence. Someone had to say...something.

"I think I'm going to run to the ladies' room before we have dessert." She hopped up from her chair. "I'll be right back."

Liza jumped up as well. "That's a good idea. Save us some cheesecake. We'll be back in a few minutes. I need to freshen up my lipstick."

In the summer, dessert was always served on the back terrace as long as the weather was good.

Liza linked her arm with Mariah and practically dragged her out of the dining room. On second thought, maybe it was a bad idea to leave Ryan alone with his parents.

"Perhaps I should go back," Mariah whispered, glancing over her shoulder. "Ryan might need me to run interference."

"Mike will do it. Besides, it's not your job anymore, remember?"

She did, but it wasn't easy. Having Ryan in the same room, sitting right next to her, overrode all the good reasons they weren't together.

And they were good reasons. She had lots of them.

If only she could think of a couple…

Wait. She had one.

He was a stubborn jerk about his parents, and he needed a sharp kick to his shin. She just might be the person to do it, too.

CHAPTER NINETEEN

THIS WAS ONE of those nights when Ryan barely recognized himself. Everything had been going smoothly at dinner and then…bam. Tense words were exchanged. This time he couldn't blame it on his father. This was all on him. He'd escalated the situation and ruined everyone's digestion.

He simply couldn't seem to stop himself from saying something that would piss his dad off. Of course, Jack didn't truly know if Skip was aware of Brad's gambling but if that's what his father wanted to believe, who was Ryan to knock over that apple cart? He should have just let it go but he hadn't, opening his big mouth instead and challenging his old man.

Jack Beck never backed down from a challenge. Neither did Ryan.

It looked like Mariah had been right about that one. He had quite a bit in common with his dad after all. In fact, Mariah had been correct about a lot of things, including that Ryan wasn't blameless for the tension between him and his parents. Looking back, he'd carried at least half of the load. Jack and Patricia were only fifty percent to blame. Now he had a hell of a lot of thinking to do about the relationship with his parents. If he could change a bit…let things go…

Everything always had to be your way. You couldn't compromise, ever.

Mariah's words haunted him. She'd told him when they'd broken up, and then she'd told him again that first night he'd been in her apartment. How many times did he need to hear it before he believed it?

A whole bunch, apparently.

He had changed over the years but when he was back with his parents it was like he was a kid again. And he was acting like it. He needed to straighten up and act like the man he professed to be. He didn't know how he was going to fix his tattered relationship with his mom and dad, but at least now he knew he wanted to.

Realization had hit him between the eyes and that's the only explanation for why he was now standing in the middle of his childhood bedroom. It wasn't like he hadn't seen it in years. He didn't stay in it when he visited for the holidays – that's what the apartment was for – but it was a handy place to retreat to when family get-togethers became a little too much.

Tonight, however, it felt like he was seeing this room through fresh eyes.

His parents hadn't changed much, if anything from when he'd moved out during college. His sports trophies were still sitting on the shelf above his desk, and his favorite books sat on the bookcase. A quick swipe of his finger down the oak surface told him that the housekeepers were cleaning his room even though he wasn't here. The shelves, books, and trophies were completely dust free.

So many memories crowded his brain as he stood there, taking his past all in. Images of Liza and himself, hiding in his room to wrap Christmas presents, long nights sitting at the old computer studying, and his friends crowding in on his sixteenth birthday to play video games and eat pizza. He wouldn't mind traveling back for a day or two, just to feel like a kid again, when everything seemed possible and worries were what grownups had.

"What are you doing in here?"

Ryan turned at the voice but he already knew who it was. Mariah. She'd come looking for him, and to be honest, he'd expected it.

Shit, who was he kidding? He was hoping for it.

Because of all the images that kept running through his brain the most technicolor were of Mariah in this room, laughing and happy. *They'd been happy.* When had it all changed?

"I needed space," he finally replied when she didn't say anything else.

She walked into the room, quietly closing the door behind her. "They're wondering where you are."

"I know. I just wanted some quiet for a few minutes."

Stepping back, she reached for the doorknob. "I can leave you—"

"No," he interjected swiftly. "I don't want you to go."

"You want me to stay?"

She seemed confused by his statement. He didn't blame her in the least. He was pretty fucking confused himself, but at this moment he wanted her with him.

"I want you to stay."

"Okay." She came to stand by him, her gaze on the bookshelf he was studying. "Are we looking for something in particular?"

Yes, but not a book.

"I'm looking for where it all changed. Can you tell me when that happened because I just don't know."

"What are you thinking changed?"

"Everything. We were happy together and then we weren't. Apparently, it was because I'm a total asshole and have to have everything my way. I can see that now and I thought I'd changed these past years. I thought I was better. Then tonight happened and I think that maybe I haven't changed at all."

She turned toward him, placing her hand on his arm to tug him so they were looking into each other's eyes. He had vivid memories of staring into those bright green and gold orbs on more than one occasion. When Mariah was happy, they'd turn a dark forest green and when she was aroused, they'd turn more golden. Those memories were keenly sharp. He could easily recall every freckle and mole on her satiny soft skin. He'd kissed every one of them more times than he could count. Where they still there?

I want to know.

"You're not an asshole and you have changed."

"You can't know that. I've only been home a few days."

She shook her head and smiled. "The Ryan Beck I knew and loved before would never have asked these introspective questions about himself. He never would have doubted whether he was doing or saying the right thing. He was always supremely sure of himself at all times. It could be very annoying."

"I don't annoy you now?"

"You do, but in completely new and different ways."

The way she said it, lovingly and not in the least bit pissed off, had him laughing. She had always been funny along with challenging and even now she wasn't giving him an out. She still held him accountable for his bullshit.

"I hope those new ways are better than the past ones."

"They are." She tugged at his shirt sleeve. "Will you cut yourself some slack? You have changed, Ryan. More than I ever thought possible. But I think you expect perfection. Wait, that was a stupid statement. I don't think it, I know it. I know that you expect perfection from yourself but that might be a tad unrealistic since you're, you know, human and all. You're allowed to have some flaws as long as being a sociopathic killer isn't one of them."

"You make me sound like a fucking mess."

She softly laughed. "You haven't figured it out yet, have you? Ryan, we're all a mess. Every single one of us. We're all just trying to get through life without ripping our hair out and retreating into our rooms to draw pretty pictures with non-toxic crayons. You're not special. You're just as screwed up as the rest of us. Welcome to life. Once you let go of your delusions of perfection, you'll be a hell of a lot happier. I know that everyone around you will be a lot happier."

"My parents aren't a mess."

His statement was pure instinct but after the words left his mouth he had to wonder if they were even true. When he was younger, he would have said that they were.

"Naw, they're just better at hiding it than most people. Just like you are. Do you honestly think that they didn't doubt themselves when they were younger and raising two kids? I bet they did, but they didn't want you or anyone else to know. They probably lost a night or two of sleep wondering if they were making the right decisions."

"I can't even imagine it."

"Can't you? Really? Do you honestly believe that your parents just know what they do is right and never have any doubt at all?"

It did sound rather far-fetched. Humans had doubts.

"I guess I've just never seen it."

"Because they didn't want you to. Especially when we're young, our parents want us to think that they know everything and can fix everything. It's when we become adults that we realize that our parents aren't perfect. But we love them anyway. Assuming, of course, that they haven't been abusive or anything. I'm talking regular, run of the mill parental units here."

Ryan had never considered his parents run of the mill or

ordinary. To him they had always been almost superhuman, definitely above average. The fact that they made him crazy didn't change that.

"I do love my parents. They can just get under my skin."

"Because they don't act the way you want them to."

He was too ashamed to agree out loud, but Mariah had to know that she'd spoken the truth.

"You wanted them to be different," she continued on. "You wanted them to be huggy, emotional parents that made brownies and helped you build blanket forts."

"I didn't even know what a blanket fort was until you told me. I think I was thirteen or fourteen at the time."

"That's not child abuse, Ryan. They loved you." She stepped back and her gaze swept around the room. "Look at your bedroom. It's a shrine to your childhood. They haven't changed a thing. Not one thing. It's like a time capsule here. Do you think they didn't change it because they're lazy or didn't have the cash to redecorate? No, they did it because they love you. They love you and I bet they think about your childhood a lot. I bet when they're alone they reminisce about funny stuff that you and Liza did when you were little. It's just not their way to do that out in the open. I know you want it to be different, but you need to accept them as they are."

"They don't accept me," Ryan shot back. He remembered too many arguments with his mom and dad about him becoming a cop. "They hate my job."

"Are you doing your job to get your parents' approval or are you doing it for you?"

"For me."

"Then it doesn't matter, does it? If you're not going to change your job then the whole conversation is moot. Yet, you still let them get you all wound up about it. Ryan, they don't expect you to change your career. When was the last time they bugged out about joining the family business? How long has it been?"

Years. He couldn't really remember the exact time.

"A while ago. But they weren't thrilled about my latest job change," he protested. "They weren't happy about that."

"They were just disappointed. They'd hoped you would come home if you took a new job." She moved right in front of him, and he could smell the teasing scent of her perfume. They were close enough that he could feel the heat from her body penetrating the thin cotton of his shirt. "I was disappointed that you didn't come home."

That hit him in the chest – right in the spot where his heart resided. He'd thought about her so many times even when he hadn't wanted to. That she had thought about him too made him...glad.

"Chicago isn't home anymore," he admitted honestly. "But I did think about you, Mariah. More than I should have."

He'd gotten blind drunk the night of her wedding. He'd told himself it didn't have anything to do with her, he'd simply wanted to go out and have some fun.

He was a lying sack of crap.

"More than I should have," she echoed. "Yes, that's true for me. It seems like you were always around, everywhere I looked."

"I know the feeling. You're in every nook and cranny of this room," he said, keeping his voice low. For some reason they were whispering as if they were confessing deep dark secrets and someone had their ear pressed against the door outside. "I have so many memories of you and me here."

Almost all of them were steamy, and some downright filthy. Sure, there was plenty of hanging out and watching television, but to be honest he'd been the stereotypical horn dog teenage boy. Just having Mariah in the same room with him was enough to turn even the most innocent of meetings into a hot make-out session. They'd had issues when they were together, but their physical intimacy wasn't one of them. It had always been so good with her.

She had to be having the same thoughts because the temperature in his old bedroom had risen at least fifty degrees in the last five minutes and he was beginning to sweat on the back of his neck. His heart was beginning to bang against his ribs as well, the blood pumping through his veins. It was amazing that this woman could get him like this without even trying, but then it had always been that way.

She was...special. There would never be another woman like Mariah. It was time he admitted that to himself.

Fuck, it was time he admitted a hell of lot of things to himself. He'd been lying and almost believing it for far too long. Time to strip away all of the bullshit and come clean.

"Mariah, I–"

The words stuck in his too-tight throat. He didn't know what to say because he barely knew what he was feeling. Was this nostalgia or something more? Something...new? In the last few days he'd been blown away by the sheer magnificence of this woman before him. She'd always been formidable, but now? She was amazing.

It was more than just her looks, although she was incredibly gorgeous. It was the way she stood up to him, not letting him get away with anything. She wasn't in the least impressed with him and yet he knew that she had feelings for him as well. He could see it in her green eyes, currently bright with unshed tears.

She felt it, too. This riptide of emotion that was almost pulling him under with its undeniable force. He could only do one thing.

He reached out and pulled her into his arms.

She didn't resist. Quite the contrary, she pressed herself against him, every curve tucked neatly against him. His head spun as her scent filled his nostrils. It wasn't flowery because that wasn't Mariah. This aroma was something akin to witchcraft. Musky, but subtle, with hints of spice. His hands slid down her spine as he pressed his face into the hollow of her shoulder and inhaled deeply into his aching lungs. If he lived to be a hundred and fifty, he'd never forget the heady way she smelled. Blue jeans and t-shirt or expensive evening gown, it was always the same.

Mariah.

"Ryan," she whispered when his lips found that spot at the

base of her neck that he knew drove her crazy with need. Her fingers tightened on his biceps as he nibbled at the velvety skin. "More."

She never needed to ask. He'd give her anything she wanted.

He left a trail of kisses over her jaw and to her mouth, her lips parting instantly to give him access. She tasted of coffee and chocolate and Mariah.

At some point, they must have drifted across the room in each other's arms because they were now lying on his childhood bed, like so many times before, only this time he was a grown man and she didn't have to be home by midnight. He could make love to her all night long.

"Oh my God! I knew it! You two are back together."

He'd been so lost in kissing Mariah that he hadn't heard the click of the door or noticed the shaft of light from the hallway. Dragging his lips from hers, he lifted his head to snarl a reply to his nosy sister Liza but Mariah beat him to it. She pushed at his shoulders so he had to roll away and she sat up, fussing with the neckline of her sundress.

"Liza, I love you like a sister. I'd take a bullet for you, but if you don't get the hell out of this bedroom immediately, I'm going to tell Mike that you had strippers at your bachelorette party."

There was a giggle and Liza slapped her hand over her mouth, but she backed out of the room and the door snapped shut. They were alone again.

But the mood was gone. In its place was an uneasiness, a

pesky tension. It was different than before but no less madden-
ing. Ryan once again didn't know what to say, so he said the first
thing that popped into his head.

"I didn't know Liza had strippers at her bachelorette party."

"She didn't. But it wouldn't stop me from telling Mike
that."

"You play dirty."

"Did you want her to hang around and try and get us to talk
about our relationship?"

That sounded like pure hell.

"Fuck, no."

"Then you're welcome."

Levering up from the mattress, he sat next to her on the bed.
"So what do we do now?"

He had a few ideas and in most of them they were horizon-
tal. But he wasn't fussy. Up against the wall would be fine, too.

"We straighten our clothes, wipe the lipstick off of your face,
and then go downstairs and try to pretend that we weren't
pawing at each other for the last fifteen minutes."

That wasn't the answer he was hoping for.

"What did you think we were going to do?" she said with a
short laugh. "Just continue on? Your parents probably have a
decent idea as to why we both disappeared. It's going to be
embarrassing as it is when we go downstairs."

He hadn't really thought about his parents.

"I'm not really thinking straight at the moment. Too little
blood in my brain cells. And please don't mention my parents at

a time like this. They don't help matters."

Giggling, she stood and walked over to the mirror hanging on the wall. Snapping on the desk lamp, she fluffed her hair and tugged at her clothing.

"Does mentioning your mommy dampen your…enthusiasm?"

"Hell, yes. So stop, okay?"

She turned then, a smile playing on her kiss-swollen lips. His parents were definitely going to notice that she looked ravished.

"I'm doing it on purpose. Do you want to go downstairs with…that?" With a smirk, she pointed at his tented trousers. "You'll scare them to death."

It was good that they could laugh about this. Right?

"You have a point. Maybe we should wait a minute or two."

With her standing there looking amazing, it wasn't easy to cool down, though.

"Do you want me to help some more? We can talk about the time you jumped in that ice-cold lake in the mountains. Remember how cold that was?"

Ball-shriveling cold.

"That did it. I'm good." He stood and realized that she'd managed to get a few of his shirt buttons undone. "Let's go downstairs, make some excuse so we can get out of here, then go back to your place and pick up where we left off."

She simply laughed at him. "Do you honestly think that it's going to be that easy? Your sister is downstairs."

Shit. Liza wasn't going to let this go. They both had to walk downstairs and deal with her. She'd probably already told his parents and called a justice of the peace for an impromptu wedding ceremony.

He'd kissed Mariah and now everything was different.

He just didn't know how different. Or what this all meant.

They needed to figure it out before they faced his family. Except that Mariah was already opening the door and heading into the hallway. Too late to talk.

For a moment, he contemplated turning the other direction and sneaking out of the back door but that wasn't an option. He had to go downstairs and act confident, as if everything was normal and not a big deal.

But kissing Mariah was a big damn deal.

And he wanted to do it again.

CHAPTER TWENTY

MARIAH DIDN'T SAY much to Ryan when they joined his family out on the back terrace. She didn't say much when she bid them goodbye either. She didn't say a single word on the drive back to the apartment.

The plain truth was she didn't know what to say.

She'd wanted to kiss Ryan. She could admit that to herself. She'd been thinking about it since he'd returned to Chicago and, to be honest, their encounter in his childhood bedroom had been inevitable. There was simply too much chemistry between the two of them to ignore. It had always been there and had never dimmed, although she'd been shocked by how it had intensified. His mere touch was electric.

She didn't regret kissing him either. He was a damn fine kisser and if anything had only become more skilled since their last make-out session.

But...this was more than a kiss. This was a big deal.

It could never be casual between them and they both knew that. There wouldn't be any hooking up and then saying goodbye a few days or weeks later as if what happened didn't matter.

It did matter. *They* mattered. They'd crossed over a line tonight and while she didn't want to go backward, she sure as hell didn't know what was ahead. Were they both really ready to try again? She wanted a second chance with him, but it wasn't going to be easy. They had over a decade and a thousand miles between them. It would be hard work to bridge that gap.

It would be worth it, but they both had to be all in. No half measures. Watching him walk out of her life again would be too painful. It had been hard enough the first time.

To his credit, Ryan didn't try and get her to talk much, letting the silence settle uncomfortably between them. They both knew they were going to have to talk eventually but it was good to try and wrangle all the thoughts and emotions into something moderately coherent.

If he's not all in, it will be okay. I'll survive. Heartbroken, but okay. I'll move on.

Her life had been perfectly fine before he'd returned, and it could be fine again. It would be better with Ryan in it but that might not be an option.

She unlocked her apartment door and dropped her purse and keys on the kitchen counter, Ryan on her heels.

"Do you want a glass of wine?"

He shook his head. "Not really. Do you want to slap my face?"

Straight to the point. It was a relief, honestly. No circling the topic or beating around the bush. They'd just get down to it. It was the best way.

"No. Is that something you're into now? Getting slapped? Because that's not my kink."

Ryan threw back his head and laughed, which was exactly what she'd hoped he would do. It helped ease the wall of tension that had built up between them on the way home.

"Sassy as ever, babe. That's what I love about you. And no, that isn't my kink either. I was just wondering if you were feeling that I took advantage of you. I made the first move."

"And I made the second," Mariah replied, settling into the corner of the couch and tucking her bare feet under her. "I have no regrets."

"That's good."

They stared at one another for a long moment, neither one wanting to be the next to speak. This was the tricky part.

Sighing, she rolled her eyes. "So…talk to me. We kissed. Do you want to do it again? Because I do."

"Hell, yes. Of course I want to do it again."

He was still standing in the middle of the living room.

"But we need to talk," she finally said. "We need to decide if it's a good idea. If we can really do this."

His shoulders slumped slightly. "I want to make this work, Mariah. I'm just going to take a leap of faith and put that out there. I've never been able to get you out of my head or my heart. I want a second chance. What about you?"

He'd been brave and now she had to do the same. Her heart was pounding and her hands were shaking so hard she had to tuck them under her knees. For all her jokes and bravado, she was scared shitless. It was like jumping off a cliff and praying that someone below had accidentally left a mattress behind to break your fall.

There were no guarantees. They'd grown up but had they changed enough? She didn't have the answer.

"I want that, too," she said, sounding almost breathless which wasn't surprising. She was almost dizzy just sitting here from lack of oxygen. "I'm scared, though."

He shoved his hands in his pockets. "Me, too. I don't want to fuck this up. I want this to work, Mariah."

"But...?"

"No buts. I want this to work and I'm willing to do what it takes. I just–"

He broke off just as Mariah had finally taken a deep breath.

"So there is a but."

"I don't want us to fall into old habits. We've both changed. I just want it to be enough."

At least they had the same fears. It would be easier to face them together.

"Can I tell you something that I learned from my marriage and divorce?"

"Yes, as long as it's not how much you loved and adored him."

Rubbing at her temple, she shook her head. "I learned that no matter what you do or how hard you work, if you're not with the right person it's not going to be okay. Bobby and I did everything that we were supposed to do. We went to marriage counseling. We did all the homework, we went on date nights, and we shared our feelings. Ultimately, it didn't matter because we just weren't right for one another."

He gave her a dubious look. "I'm not sure what you're saying here."

"I guess what I'm saying is that I think that you're the right person."

It was scary saying it out loud. They'd been apart a long time.

"I think that you are, too," he said softly. "I want to make this work. I don't want to walk away and wonder what might have happened."

She didn't either.

"You don't live in Chicago."

She wasn't sure why she was bringing up that fact at this particular moment. It was just one of a myriad of issues that they'd face in the future. Perhaps she wanted to see right here and right now if he'd compromise. He'd had trouble with that before.

"I don't," he agreed. "That's going to be an issue. I can talk to my bosses about possibly working out of Chicago. I don't know if they'll agree to it, but I can try."

"You would do that?"

"I can only try. If they say no, then I'll have to travel back and forth. I would hope you would travel, too."

"I would." She nodded, her mind going a million miles an

hour. He'd done it. He was capable of compromise. She could almost hear angels singing. "I might consider moving to Seattle, if you can't move here."

His brows shot up. "You'd leave Chicago? You love it here."

She almost opened her mouth to tell him that she loved him too, but it was too soon to be making emotional declarations. They had much to work out.

"I won't ask you to make all of the compromises. It wouldn't be fair."

"Careful," he chuckled. "We're almost sounding like a mature couple. We don't want to get too crazy."

"We do sound mature. How boring," Mariah teased. "Next thing you know we'll be discussing the weather and fire insurance."

"Fire insurance is important," he agreed with mock solemnity. "And I think it's supposed to rain tomorrow."

They both burst into laughter, the weird tension between them starting to drain away. They knew each other so well. Her date had been right. It didn't matter that they'd been apart for over a decade. They had a history together. She knew that he didn't like black olives and he knew that she cried easily when watching movies or television. She knew that Christmas was his favorite holiday and he knew that Halloween was hers. They knew the deep stuff, too – the fears and the dreams. She wanted to learn all about any new dreams he might have, too.

"I like the rain. I just don't like storms," she replied. It was inane but they were both just gazing at each other sort of stupidly. She wanted to stand up and run into his arms but she wasn't sure what the next step was.

Luckily, Ryan appeared to know what to do at momentous moments like this. He stepped forward, a smile playing on his handsome face.

"Can I kiss you again?"

She wanted that. More than she wanted to breathe.

Her heart raced and her hands trembled with emotion. She'd never admitted it to herself but this was what she'd wanted. Ryan.

Gathering every bit of courage she had, she answered his question.

"Only if you make love to me, too."

From the grin on his face, she was pretty sure his answer was yes.

CHAPTER TWENTY-ONE

MARIAH DIDN'T REMEMBER making a conscious decision to move into the bedroom with Ryan but somehow that's where they'd ended up. Rolling around on her mattress, they couldn't seem to get enough of one another, their hands constantly touching, exploring, and pulling at clothes that were simply in the way.

There was a confidence in Ryan that he hadn't had the last time they were together. Not that he hadn't been sure of himself...he had been. But now it was different. It was the quieter, more mature confidence of a man that was comfortable in his skin. There was no hesitation and there was also no haste. The sex with him had always been good but she could already tell that this time was going to be amazing. His fingers seemed to find all of the most sensitive spots on her body and his mouth and tongue were doing dangerously delicious things as well. It was so good and it was only the beginning. If they played their cards right, they'd get to do this together over and over again for years to come.

She liked the sound of that. Together. For years. This man

had owned her heart for so long. It was only fair that she owned his as well.

Their clothes were in a forgotten heap on the floor as Ryan kissed a wet trail down her neck and between her breasts. The pads of his thumbs stroked her peaked nipples until she was twisting under him, soft sighs escaping from her lips.

"Ryan," she whispered, her heavy lids fluttering closed.

She heard his chuckle and then his tongue glided across her flesh, up and down, back and forth, making her reach out and clutch the back of his head so that his mouth would go where she needed him the most. His lips closed around her nipple, the teeth slightly scraping and sending a rush of arousal through her veins and to the tips of her curled toes.

Her fingers dug into his scalp as she writhed against the sheets, a bar of arousal beginning to form in her abdomen. She could hear the pounding of her heart as if a drum had taken up residence in her skull, picking up speed with every beat.

Kissing his way down her belly, he nudged her legs apart with his wide shoulders. His tongue traced patterns on the sensitive skin of her inner thigh before traveling to her core. A shiver ran up her spine and her breath caught in her throat. Part of her wanted to scream his name and the other part wanted to sigh in pure ecstasy. She wasn't sure which side was going to win but she was leaning toward screaming at the top of her lungs. It had always been good but this time it was...more. They were more themselves so they could be more to each other.

His warm lips pressed baby kisses against the slick flesh, and then he pressed a thick digit inside of her, swirling his finger against the hidden spots that only served to send her flying higher into the clouds. His tongue did wickedly naughty things on the outside while his fingers stroked from the inside, setting up a situation that was only going to end up one way.

With an almighty explosion.

Mariah fell over the edge with Ryan's name on her lips. She squeezed her eyes shut as her climax took control but that didn't stop her from seeing stars or feeling the world tilt on its axis. It also didn't stop her from clutching at his shoulders, something to steady herself when everything was spinning and whirling in her brain.

When it was over, she opened her eyes to see him quietly lying beside her, his blue gaze taking in every detail. With any other human being she would have been embarrassed, hiding her face, but with Ryan it was different. She wanted to reveal the secrets of her soul to him, and she wanted to learn his as well.

"That looked like fun," he finally said when the world had stopped spinning like a top. His breath was warm on her cheek. "Want to do it again?"

"You haven't even done it once yet," she said, her hand cupping cheek, his jaw stubbled against her palm. Her heart ached with such love for this man that had returned to her life. How had she ever made it through without him? She only felt truly whole when they were together. She'd simply been walking through life these last few years pretending to be completely alive. "Maybe we should take care of that first."

"We can take care of both of us at the same time."

Oh, that sounded like a good plan. Why didn't I think of that?

Because I can't think straight when we're naked like this.

A naked Ryan Beck was a sight to behold. He'd filled out in the last decade, his shoulders wider, his legs more muscular, his skin golden. His stomach was still just as flat and she couldn't stop herself from reaching out and running her fingertips over the ridged abdomen. The muscles under her palm jerked and jumped in response and she heard the sharp intake of his breath.

"What are you up to, baby?" He tangled a hand in her hair and pulled her in for a long, hard kiss that left her barely able to form words.

"I'm just…exploring."

Rolling onto his back, Ryan gave her a wolfish grin. "Then go for it. I'm all yours."

This sounds interesting.

All mine.

At one point in her life, Mariah might have hesitated. Not this time. She wanted to enjoy and savor every single moment of their reunion. Levering from the bed, she straddled Ryan so she was looking down at him from her lofty perch above.

And the view was mighty fine indeed. She wasn't sure where she wanted to start. There were so many options and all of them good.

He waggled his brows in challenge. "What are you waiting for?"

She tapped her chin. "I'm just deciding. Don't rush me."

"Far be it for me to hurry you along. I'll just wait here and do nothing."

She ran her fingernails lightly down his torso, eliciting a groan. "Don't be sarcastic. This is serious business here."

"Of course. Strictly business. Carry on then."

That was exactly what she was going to do.

As if she had all the time in the world, she let her hands glide all over his chest, stomach, and arms, delighting in every sigh and groan from his lips. She loved how his muscular body was so different than her own, and she savored the sensation of his skin against hers. The soft sprinkling of golden-brown hair on his arms and chest, and then that treasure trail that led from belly button to his cock. Once her hands were done exploring, she took her lips on the same adventure across his heated flesh, finding even more sensitive spots that she'd never knew existed.

She was heading farther south when the world suddenly turned on its side and the breath was knocked out of her lungs.

Somehow, Ryan had lifted up from the mattress and flipped her onto her back. Now he was the one straddling her body wearing an evil genius smile on his face. He leaned down so they were almost nose to nose, his hands on either side of her head.

"Since this is serious business, I think it's about time to get down to it. I don't think I can wait anymore."

She could feel him hot, hard, and ready against her thigh.

I don't want to wait anymore either.

She's already waited ten years. One more minute just might kill her.

"I'm on the pill," she blurted out, suddenly realizing that they weren't kids anymore. They had to act like adults. Even back then they'd been careful. "You know...for my periods. It helps."

She'd had awful, painful cycles until her doctor had found the right pill to help alleviate the symptoms.

"I'm clean," he replied. "And healthy. But I don't have an issue wearing a condom if you want me to. We can get tested together so we don't have to later."

Do I have condoms? Yes, I do.

Liza had bought a box for Mariah after the divorce. It was shoved under the sink in the bathroom because frankly, she hadn't been thinking much about sex after the divorce.

"I have condoms in the bathroom. Liza bought them for me."

"That sounds like my sister. No need to go that far. I think I have one in my wallet."

He quickly took care of the foil packet and then laid on top of her, his weight on his elbows. His lips brushed her cheek and jaw, nuzzling her ear.

"Are you ready for me, sweetheart? Are you sure about this?"

"Yes, I'm sure. I don't want to wait anymore."

He started slowly, pressing forward inch by delicious inch and running over those hidden spots again. By the time he was in to the hilt she could have sworn she could see stars and the world was tilting again. Heat swept over her body, and an impatience took control. She wanted him now. She needed him *now.* She trusted Ryan with everything she was. She knew he'd never hurt her.

Because he never had.

"More," she panted, her nails scoring the skin on his shoulders, urging him to move. "Don't go slow. You know how I like it."

He remembered it all. How she liked it when he scooped her knees over his elbows so he could thrust harder and faster. The way she loved to feel a little helpless. His rough cheek against her neck, his teeth nibbling at her shoulder. She whispered filthy words of encouragement that she'd never spoken with any other man. She let him take control and he didn't disappoint, their rhythm sending the two of them over the cliff.

When they finally came down, sucking oxygen into their starved lungs, Ryan fell onto his back, pulling him with her so she was tucked into his side. She pillowed her head on his chest, loving the steady thump of his heart under her ear. It was so right, so solid, so safe and warm. She never wanted to move from here, content to live the rest of her life in this bed with this man.

They'd have to order food in, of course.

She was drifting in and out of sleep, Ryan's fingers stroking her skin when she heard it.

The words.

She hadn't known how much she wanted them until she heard them.

"I love you, Mariah."

The sting of tears behind her closed eyelids matched the ache in her chest. Licking her lips, the words fell easily from her tongue. She didn't want him to think for one minute that she didn't feel the same.

"I love you, too."

They would work it all out. It wouldn't be easy, but it would be worth it.

Ryan was worth it.

IT WAS THE same old story. Ryan couldn't sleep.

He ought to be sawing logs with Mister Sandman after making love with Mariah, but even amazing sex with the love of his life hadn't managed to put him out. His mind was simply too active, constantly keeping him up when most of the world was out like a light. Luckily, he was used to it and honestly, he didn't need much sleep. He could easily function on three or four hours. While Mariah slumbered peacefully, he'd try to get some work done. There was always a never-ending list of reports to do.

"Some things never change."

He heard her soft voice before he saw her. He was going through the emails on his phone when her bare feet came into his line of sight. His gaze rose to take her all in and his heart tumbled in his chest. How on earth had he lived one single minute without her?

She looked absolutely adorable. All sleepy and mussed. Her long dark hair in a riot around her shoulders with a few stray strands sticking up in the back. Mariah's hair had a tendency to curl and a couple were clinging to her creamy cheeks as if for dear life. Wearing a tank top and striped sleep shorts, she yawned and rubbed at her eyes.

"You're awake again. Do you ever sleep?"

"I sleep. Just not as much as you do."

Mariah loved to sleep. She had always extolled the virtues of eight solid hours of sack time a night. Ryan didn't think he'd slept that much even as a child. It simply wasn't in his DNA.

"I don't know how you do it," she replied, settling down on the couch next to him and cuddling close. She was still warm from being wrapped up in the bedcovers, and he placed his phone on the side table so he could pull her even closer. "I would be a walking zombie if I didn't sleep most of the time."

"I'm used to it. I've actually learned to be glad about it over the years. I can stay up and get work done, if I need to, or read or watch television. It's sometimes nice to be awake when the rest of the world is asleep. It's quiet and peaceful."

She rested her head on his shoulder. "Do you want me to leave you alone then?"

"No," he laughed. "I like having your company. You can sit here with me as long as you like."

"I like your company, too." She paused for a moment, but Ryan could tell that she wasn't finished speaking. She had something to say. "I'm not sorry that we did that."

Ah, they were going to have *the talk.*

"I'm not sorry either."

Another long pause.

"Did you mean what you said?"

"About what?"

"Maybe moving back here."

She thought he wasn't serious about making compromises. Time to let her know that he really had changed.

"I meant it. I want this to work between the two of us. It's now one of my main priorities."

Her fingertips skittered over his arm. "I don't know that I've ever been a priority to you. This will be interesting."

That was his fault. He hadn't been good at showing her, but then he'd been too young to know what to do. Hopefully, he had a better idea now.

"I'm sorry that I made you feel that way. Truly sorry. I want you to believe that you're important to me, Mariah. I want you to believe that we can make this work."

"I do believe it."

A little bit. But she wasn't completely convinced.

"We both need to see the change in action. We're different now, and we're still going to make some mistakes. At least I am, but I'm willing to acknowledge them and try to do better."

"I want to do better, too," she vowed, sitting up so she could look directly at him. "I think I'd like to come out to where you live and look around a bit. Spend some time there. Maybe…maybe I'll move to you instead of you moving here."

"I think you'd love Seattle, but it's okay if you don't. We'll figure it out. We don't have to make all the decisions tonight."

"Thank goodness, because I'm fuzzy from lack of sleep."

He didn't get a chance to reply. His phone buzzed, pulling him away briefly to check who would be sending him a text at two in the morning.

Logan, of course. He didn't sleep either, plus it was earlier in Seattle. Ryan quickly read through the message, his heart in his throat.

"You just got a strange look on your face," Mariah said. "Can I ask what's going on?"

Ryan didn't answer until he'd read through the message a second time. He needed to be sure that he'd understood it correctly.

"It's a message from my boss Logan. Apparently, someone has confessed to Brad's murder. A guy in state prison. Logan wants me to go talk to him tomorrow." Then Ryan remembered that it was past midnight in Chicago. "I mean today. He's not sure that this person isn't just looking for a few minutes of fame, but we have to check every lead."

"That's good. You may be able to close the case. The Harrington family will be relieved."

This would be closure for them, and for Ryan and his friends as well.

Is that what happened to you, Brad? Were you killed by a stranger?

Morning couldn't come fast enough. Ryan wanted to talk to this person. He wanted to know what happened that night.

CHAPTER TWENTY-TWO

RYAN WAS GETTING dressed in his own apartment the next morning when he heard a banging on the door. He'd just left Mariah less than half an hour ago, popping into his own place to shower and change, so he didn't think it could be her. She'd said something about working in her studio and then later having lunch with Liza.

"Just a minute," he called out as the banging continued. "Jesus, give it a break."

This building had a locked front door. How had someone slipped in?

One look out of the peephole had him chuckling. He should have known.

Knox Owens – one of his coworkers.

For all Ryan knew, the guy had crawled up the side of the building and swung in an open window. He was that crazy.

"You're making a hell of a racket," Ryan said when he opened the door. "A simple knock would have done it."

"Apparently not," Knox said, walking into the apartment, carrying a small suitcase. "I did knock but no one answered. So I knocked louder."

"I might not have been here."

"Jared pinged your phone. You were here."

That was the problem with working with investigators. They had tricks up their sleeves.

"I was in the shower. I'm about to make some coffee. Do you want some?"

Knox grinned and sat down at the kitchen island. "Hook me up to an IV. I couldn't sleep on the plane. The people around me were all snoring. Damn, they were loud. I wouldn't mind some breakfast either, if you were making some for yourself. I'm starving."

Knox was always starving.

Ryan retrieved the coffee from the cabinet. "Not that I'm not happy to see you, but why are you here? I thought they were going to send Luke."

Pretending to be hurt, Knox placed his hand over his heart and sighed. "Wow, that was a sharp stick in the eye. Am I not good enough?"

"You're good enough. You're just a surprise."

"Luke's all tangled up in a case. I wrapped up mine yesterday so they put me on the red-eye. No rest for the wicked."

"I appreciate you coming out," Ryan said, cracking eggs into a bowl. "Hope you like scrambled eggs because that's all I can do with them."

"No problem. Can I do anything to help?"

"I got it. There's yogurt and fruit in the refrigerator if you want something more healthy and I have bread for toast. I even have strawberry jam to go on it."

Courtesy of Liza's grocery run.

"That all sounds good."

They didn't talk much as they devoured their food. Knox filled him in on what was going on at the office, and Ryan talked about the status of the case.

"So we're going to the prison today?" Knox asked, getting up to rinse his plate. Clearly, he was going to be a good guest. His mama had trained him right. "Do you think this guy did it?"

"I have no idea," Ryan replied. "I've never had a case blown wide open with an out of the blue confession from someone that wasn't even a suspect. It seems a little too easy, if you ask me, but it would be great if this were the answer to all of my unanswered questions. I'm just not sure that I'm that lucky."

"Do we need a plan when we talk to him? How will we know his confession is real?"

Ryan drained his coffee cup and then checked his watch. They needed to get on the road. It was a long drive.

"According to the coroner, Brad was killed with a piece of metal pipe that was found next to his body. It fit the fracture of the skull perfectly. That information has never been released to the public, though. If this guy did it, he's going to know about the pipe. The public only knows that it was blunt force trauma to the head."

Knox nodded approvingly. "Got it. If he doesn't have that detail it can't be him."

Ryan had borrowed Mariah's car for the drive to the prison just outside of Chicago. It was a maximum-security facility, and the man they were going to visit was already behind bars for a double murder in a convenience store robbery.

Tim Muldeen. He had a record as long as Ryan's arm, starting with petty crime when he was a teenager and graduating to more hardcore activities as he aged. He had the perfect storm of a childhood – abusive and poverty-stricken. He was in and out of foster homes, hated school, and his father used him as a punching bag.

This was what Mariah had been talking about. Ryan may not have had the perfect upbringing but he hadn't been abused in the least. His parents had done their best and he was one lucky son of a bitch to be born into the Beck family.

Tim Muldeen, on the other hand, had been dealt a losing hand from birth. It wasn't difficult to imagine the man hitting another human being with a metal pipe.

Muldeen was a murderer. But was he Brad's murderer? Only time would tell.

MARIAH KNEW SHE wasn't going to get away with not talking to Liza about what she'd seen last night so instead she decided to face it head on. She scheduled a lunch for the two of them because the sooner they talked about it, the sooner they could all move on.

She was sure that Liza was going to be thrilled about Mariah's second try with Ryan. She'd been pushing for it and now she was getting what she'd wanted for so long.

So when she sat down at the table with Liza, she didn't bother to beat around the bush.

"Yes, we're back together. We're going to give it another try."

Letting out a squeal that had heads turning in the restaurant, Liza hopped out of her chair and gave Mariah a huge hug.

"I'm so excited," she gushed, finally sitting down again. She was bouncing around in her chair though, her cheeks red with excitement. She looked like a five-year-old with a sugar-laden birthday cake. "I knew that if you two just spent a little time together that you'd see that you were meant to be. Oh my gosh, you're going to be my sister for real now."

Mariah laughed and held up her hands in a surrender motion. "Easy there, we haven't plighted our troth or anything like that. We're not planning a wedding."

"Not yet," Liza said, her eyes sparkling. "But you will be. Ryan's the marrying kind. He wants kids, too. You want kids, right? This is so wonderful. I'm going to be an auntie."

"Could you please slow down? We're just in the beginning stages of this. Don't book a church, okay? I'm not even sure that I want to get married again, and you don't know for sure that Ryan wants to get married."

"He does," Liza said, nodding knowingly. "And since when are you anti-marriage?"

"The divorce wasn't easy. I don't really want to go through

that again."

"But you and Ryan would never get a divorce."

"You have so much faith in us," Mariah chuckled. "I wish I had your optimism."

That was the thing about the Beck family. They were so gosh darn sure that they were completely right. Even Liza was that way.

"I just know both of you. Now please tell me that Ryan is going to move here and you're not planning to move to Seattle."

"That's a good question. We're not sure. I'm open to moving if I need to. He's going to talk to his bosses and see what they can do. Ultimately, I have the more portable career. I can paint and sculpt from anywhere."

Wrinkling her nose, Liza shook her head. "I don't want to hear that. I want you to stay here so we can be one big happy family."

"You and Mike could always move, too," Mariah suggested with a laugh. "I'm not sure how your parents will feel about that though."

"My parents just might buy another house in Seattle and live there part-time."

The couple loved to travel and they didn't like to stay in one place long. Having another home they could go to for a few months a year would be something Jack and Patricia would definitely do.

"Let's talk about the party," Liza said after they were served their food. "I've arranged for the birthday cake to be rolled in on a cart about eight-thirty and all sixty candles will be lit. I want the family – and that's you too – to gather around and sing before Mom blows out her candles. Then dad is going to surprise her with a diamond bracelet. He showed it to me last night. Impressive. Mom is going to love it."

"You didn't help pick it out?"

"Dad has excellent taste. But I'm betting that Mom gave him a few big hints as to what she wanted."

"It sounds great. You know we're going to be there."

"I just wanted to make sure that you were both around when the cake is served. No skipping upstairs to Ryan's old room for a little fun," Liza giggled.

It might be tempting if the party was boring…

"We'll be right by your side when it comes time to sing, although you know I'll just be mouthing the words."

Ryan had a great singing voice. Mariah couldn't carry a tune in a bucket. She was sort of like a human car alarm – hard on the ears.

"You're not that bad."

"You're just being nice. You know that I am. It's okay, I know it, too."

Liza reached out and patted Mariah's hand. "You're good at other things. I'll sing extra loud to cover up for you. Don't worry, we Becks got your back."

If everything worked out the way Mariah hoped it would, she just might become a Beck, too.

That didn't sound all that bad either.

★ ★ ★

"FUCK IT," RYAN muttered as they drove farther away from the prison. "That was a wasted trip."

"He definitely didn't do it," Knox agreed with a grimace. "He didn't know shit about that night. Not the bar, not Harrington, not the mode of death. Nothing. It looks like he was just looking for his name in the papers because he's fucking bored."

"So now we're back where we started. Nowhere."

"Hey, I'm here now to give you a hand," Knox protested with a chuckle. "Together we can get this investigation done and over with. We just need to sit down and go back over the evidence."

"What evidence? We don't really have any," Ryan reminded his friend. "This happened well over ten years ago and the one thing everyone is sure of is that Brad was acting completely normal that night."

"Then that's a clue," Knox replied. "It tells us that he wasn't expecting whatever happened. Even non-clues give us information."

Knox was right but it didn't make Ryan feel much better. This entire investigation was frustrating him. He wanted to bring the Harrington family peace but he wasn't sure that he could do it.

What if I fail?

"Are you heading to Steve Alton's next?" Knox asked.

Steve Alton was Trent's former next-door neighbor that used to sit outside on his balcony that overlooked the parking lot. It was a long shot but perhaps the guy might be able to give Trent an alibi for that night. They'd tracked him down and planned to talk to him this afternoon.

"Would you be mad at me if I asked you to talk to him? There's some personal business that I need to take care of."

The thought had just popped into Ryan's brain that very instant. It wasn't one of his better ideas either, but he didn't think he was going to be able to talk himself out of it. "I can do that." Knox gave him a sideways glance. "Is everything okay?"

"Yes, I just need to stop by my dad's office. I can meet you back at the apartment right after. I want you to meet Mariah. We can order in dinner and then go over the case."

"Sounds good. I have to meet this woman that has saved you from lonely bachelorhood all in the space of a few days. She must really be something."

"She is."

Ryan dropped Knox off in the downtown area and then headed to his dad's office a few blocks away. He wasn't quite sure what he was going to say when he got there. He just knew that he needed to see his dad. Mariah's words were running around in his head and they wouldn't give him any peace.

Gwen, his dad's longtime assistant greeted Ryan when he stepped off the elevator. She looked surprised to see him as she should. He couldn't remember the last time he'd been here. Maybe sometime in college? Definitely not in the last several years.

His dad was in a meeting so he cooled his heels outside chatting with Gwen for a few minutes. Her daughter had just graduated from college and was going to be a teacher in the fall, and her son was working for a law firm in the city. She'd said that Ryan's dad had been instrumental in helping him get the job.

The door to the office opened and a man exited, waving to Gwen as he left. Ryan entered, pausing just past the threshold. Suddenly, this wasn't looking like a great idea.

Why am I here? I should leave this alone. But I can't.

"Come in, son," Jack urged him. "Do you want some coffee or a pop? I can have–"

"I'm good, Dad. I just wanted to stop by."

For reasons I don't even know about.

"Have a seat." His dad sat down on the couch against the wall instead of behind his desk which was a first for Ryan. His father had always pulled the power play. "Is everything okay? Is there a problem?"

Jack looked so worried that Ryan felt shame wash over him. It was so rare that he stopped by the office to see his dad that he'd made his father think he was dying or something.

"No, everything is fine. No issues." He paused, his brain running a mile a minute. He was here for a reason. He just needed to admit it out loud. "Actually, I came by to say that I'm sorry for messing up dinner last night."

Jack Beck could have been a professional poker player. That's how close to the vest he kept his emotions most of the time. But today Ryan had clearly surprised his dad with an apology. His dad looked like he didn't know what to say.

"I didn't come here to get an apology from you," Ryan added, wondering if that's what his dad was thinking. "I just wanted to say that I'm sorry for escalating the conversation last night. It wasn't how I wanted the evening to go."

Clearing his throat a few times, Jack tugged at his silk tie. "I– I'm sorry too, son. I got a bit defensive as Pat pointed out to me later."

This was monumental. As in were pigs flying in the sky outside?

Ryan had never heard his father apologize. For anything. Ever.

For a moment, he wasn't sure that he'd heard what he'd heard. He had to replay the words in his head a few times before he could reply.

"Thank you, Dad. I promise that the next time we have dinner together it will be more friendly."

"I'll hold you to that."

Now that was a little more like the Jack Beck that Ryan knew and loved.

"How's the case going? Any progress? The newspaper this morning said that there has been a confession."

Shit, Ryan hadn't looked at the newspapers yet today. If he had, his first stop would have been Skip and Lilly instead of his dad's office.

"I wish they hadn't reported that. I talked to the guy this morning at the prison. He didn't do it. He was just bored and looking to get his name in the papers."

Looks like he'd succeeded in that.

"That's too bad. I'm sure Skip and Lilly were hopeful."

"I'm going to talk to them next."

He'd already set up a meeting with them to talk about Brad's gambling. Now they had another topic to cover as well. He felt badly that they'd had their hopes risen only to be smashed down again.

"You're going to ask them about Bradley's gambling."

Jack didn't phrase it as a question.

"Yes, I have to do that."

"I know you do. I just wish that my friends weren't going through this."

"So do I. I just hope that I can bring this investigation to some sort of conclusion."

Jack stood and walked over to the large window that over-looked downtown Chicago.

"You will. You'll find out what happened to Bradley."

"I wish I had your confidence. I'm not sure that I'll be able to do that. Cold cases are notoriously difficult to solve."

"I know that you will do your best."

His throat tightening with emotion, Ryan could barely speak. He'd never heard words like this from his father.

"Thank you for saying that. I will do my best. I hope that it's enough. I don't want to let Skip and Lilly down."

His dad cleared his throat a few more times, his gaze still out over the skyline. "You won't."

"Mariah says that you and I are a lot alike. You know…stubborn and competitive."

Ryan didn't have a clue why he'd said that, but his mouth wasn't following instructions from his brain at the moment. He was being guided by his heart instead.

Laughing, Jack smiled. "I could tell you some stories about my dad. Pat told me the same thing about me and him being just alike."

"I wouldn't mind hearing a few."

His dad checked his watch. "I've got a few minutes before my next meeting. How about I ask Gwen to bring us a couple of cold drinks and I'll tell you about the time my dad caught me smoking outside?"

Ryan wanted to hear that story. He wanted to hear them all.

CHAPTER TWENTY-THREE

KNOX HAD SENT Ryan a message that he had spoken with Steve Alton and he didn't remember anything about that night specifically. He couldn't give Trent an alibi but he also couldn't say definitely that Trent wasn't home. It was all simply too long ago.

Jared had tracked down Isla's former roommates and Knox was headed there next to talk to them. Ryan didn't hold out much hope that they'd remember anything about Brad but it was worth a shot. In the meantime, he needed to see Skip and Lilly.

Mariah knew the Harringtons as well or better than he did, and she had offered to go with him when he talked to the family, but after discussing it this morning they'd both decided it would be better for Ryan to go alone. As much as he cared about Skip and Lilly, he needed to keep a professional demeanor this afternoon. This conversation had a high probability of being emotionally charged. There was no *good* way to tell parents that their son was a gambling addict.

Seb answered the door and ushered Ryan into the living

room, just as before. Lilly and Skip once again sat on the couch while Seb perched on the arm of a chair nearby.

"Was it him? Did he do it?" Lilly asked eagerly, a wadded-up tissue in her hand. "Did he kill my baby boy?"

Ryan understood that the press had to do its job, but this would have been ten times easier if they hadn't reported that someone had confessed. They'd raised this family's hopes only to have them dashed mere hours later.

"I'm afraid not," Ryan said gently. "He didn't know any of the details that he should have known. He didn't do it."

Brows pinched together, Skip shook his head. "Then why on earth would he confess to something like that? Why would he do it?"

"Attention, probably," Ryan replied. "But he's not our guy."

Burying her head in her hands, Lilly sobbed into her tissue. "How could anyone be so cruel? To get our hopes up—"

She broke off, another sob swallowing whatever she'd been about to say. Seb immediately jumped from his spot on the chair and came to sit down next to his mother, pulling her close for comfort and patting her on the back.

"It's okay, Mom. It's going to be okay."

"I'm so sorry," Ryan replied, feeling like the worst human being in the world. He hadn't wanted anyone to cry. He was a sucker for tears. "I wish I could have better news for you, but I don't."

"Are you sure?" Skip asked, his hand seeking his wife's. "Really sure?"

"I am," Ryan said firmly. "He's not the one."

Skip gazed off into the distance for a long moment and then seemed to gather himself.

"Then it's back to the investigation," he finally said. "Have you found out anything? Anything at all?"

Having already made Lilly cry, Ryan wasn't thrilled that he was going to upset her further. But he couldn't back out. This was his job. It wasn't the first time he'd had to deliver unpleasant news but it was the first time he'd had to do it when the person wasn't a stranger.

"We have, actually. We pulled Brad's phone and bank records. It appears that he was withdrawing large sums of money on a regular basis. He was also talking to multiple bookies in both Chicago and New York. It appears that he had a gambling problem. Were you aware of that?"

He braced for the blowback.

Lilly's eyes went wide and Skip looked like someone had slapped him in the face. Seb had buried his face in his hands.

The couple exchanged a glance and then shook their heads. Lilly opened her mouth to speak but couldn't seem to get any words out, but Skip managed.

"No. No, not at all. Of course not. I can't believe that. You must be mistaken."

"I wish that we were," Ryan said softly, hating himself at the moment. He was breaking these parents' hearts. "He was definitely communicating with bookies. We know that for sure. Paired with the withdrawals and the money transfers, it looks like he was betting every single day."

Skip was already shaking his head again before Ryan even finished speaking. "I know he bet on football a little bit. Maybe when he played golf, but every day? I don't believe that."

"He made calls every day."

Skip jumped up from the couch and began to pace back and forth in front of the window.

"You have to be mistaken. Maybe his phone records got mixed up with someone else's. It was a long time ago, right? These things can happen."

"I suppose there's a small chance of that happening, but I think it's too remote to consider."

Lilly looked up from her sodden tissue, her eyes red-rimmed. "And this is why you think Bradley was killed? Because of the gambling?"

"I don't know for sure. It's something we're looking into. It's simply a possibility but it's one that we need to explore more."

She nodded as if she understood and then turned to her son. "Seb, I think I need to lie down, please."

Immediately, Seb helped her up and was shuffling her out of the living room, leaving just Ryan and Skip.

"Believe me when I say that I take no pleasure in telling you this today," Ryan said when she and Seb had gone. "But I can't do this job unless I'm completely honest with you."

"Yes–yes, I see that." Skip shoved his hands in the pockets of his trousers. "Can I ask you a question? You can answer me honestly now that Lilly isn't here. Do you think that you can really find out what happened to Brad that night? Is this case even solvable?"

It was a good question. A difficult one, too.

"To be one hundred percent honest, I don't know if I can solve this case. I've solved cases like it, but that doesn't mean that I'll be successful with this one. Cold cases are the most difficult and there isn't much physical evidence. The odds aren't in our favor but I'm going to keep working and pushing until I'm out of leads."

"And then what happens? The investigation ends?"

"Yes," Ryan admitted. "Unless some new evidence comes up, which can happen."

He wanted to give them hope, but not raise their expectations too high.

Skip stroked his chin. "That's all we can ask for. Your best. I know you're trying, Ryan. If you can't solve this, I doubt anyone could. Lilly and I may just have to learn to live with not knowing."

Ryan only wished he had better news for the family.

"What's next?" Skip asked. "Where do you go from here?"

"I'll talk to Caroline and Danny again. Maybe Theo. See if any of them noticed Brad's gambling. We'll try and talk to the bookies that he was using. If we can find them. One's in prison and the other is deceased. The latter might have had business associates that we can talk to."

"Anything else?"

"I still need to talk to Isla. She's been busy but I'm hoping to speak with her tomorrow."

Skip seemed to recognize that there wasn't much to go on. He had an utterly sad and defeated expression on his face, as if he'd aged ten years in a mere five minutes.

"Thank you for coming here and telling us in person."

"I wouldn't do anything else."

A corner of Skip's mouth quirked up. "You're a Beck, that's for sure. Your dad would have done the same."

Before yesterday Ryan wouldn't have taken that statement very well. Today? It wasn't so bad.

★   ★   ★

THE MINUTE RYAN walked into Mariah's apartment later, she knew immediately that he'd had a shitty day. He hadn't expected his meeting with the Harringtons to go well, and it looked like he was right. His shoulders were slumped and there were lines around his eyes and mouth that hadn't been there this morning.

"Shit, you look like hell," Knox said to Ryan. "I should have gone with you."

Both she and Knox had offered to accompany Ryan when he met with Lilly and Skip but he'd said that he would be better if only he were there. Knox had finished his meetings about an hour ago and he'd been sitting in her living room telling her fun stories about the cases he'd worked on with Ryan. Her man appeared to be well-liked by his coworker and for some reason that made her happy. It was clear that Knox thought that Ryan was damn good at his job.

As for Knox, she liked him. He seemed to be a straightfor-
ward guy with an optimistic nature, although serious as hell
about his job. She'd asked him if he was married or had kids and
he'd laughed loud and long. He said he wasn't the marrying kind
so she kind of got the idea that he might be a little bit of a ladies'
man. He was certainly good-looking enough to attract the
opposite sex with his dark blond hair and soft brown eyes. Plus
his grin was positively infectious. It was hard to be around him
and not be smiling, too.

"How about a beer?" she offered, not waiting for him to
reply. She grabbed one from the fridge and placed it on the
kitchen counter. "I guess it didn't go well."

"Lilly Harrington cried."

Tears. Ryan couldn't deal with a woman crying. He never
had been able to and from what she could see that hadn't
changed in the last twelve years or so. Even happy tears were
hard for him to deal with. He'd told her when they were younger
that someone crying made him feel helpless and he hated that
feeling.

Ryan took a long draw from the beer bottle before continu-
ing. "They say that they had no idea that Brad was gambling.
Actually, no. That isn't what they said. They said that they
couldn't believe it, although I assured them that Brad had been
in touch with at least two bookies. Then Lilly wanted to go lie
down, and Skip asked me if I thought I could really solve this
case."

"What did you say?" Knox asked, his smile gone for the

moment, replaced with a worried frown.

"I was honest about the odds, just as I was in the beginning. I wasn't going to sugarcoat it. It isn't going to be easy. I told him we'd work the case as long as there were leads to follow." Ryan swung his gaze to Knox. "Speaking of leads, how did your afternoon go? I hope better than mine."

"I wish I had better news," Knox said with a grimace. "Steve Alton doesn't remember that night at all. He did say that he saw Trent Aldridge come and go because his balcony was right over the parking lot, but he doesn't have any recollection of that particular night. His exact words were *'Do you know how long ago that was? Shit, I barely remember what I had for lunch yesterday. Nights that long ago all blend together.'* So, he's not going to be any help. As for Isla Foster's roommates, Jared found one still in Chicago and I went to see her."

"Let me guess, they don't remember Brad either?" Ryan said, taking another drink from the beer. "This is what happens when it's a cold case."

"They remember Brad, and they confirm that Isla was sleeping with him and that they all had some group sex a few times, but they don't know about that night in particular. They don't remember."

A muscle ticked in Ryan's jaw. "And Isla, who might remember, keeps cancelling. It's like she has something to hide from me."

Isla had always been a little different but the idea that she might have had something to do with Brad's death seemed crazy to Mariah.

"You think Isla killed Brad?"

Rubbing at his temple, Ryan shrugged. "Shit, I don't know. Not really. But she might know about his gambling. Maybe that's why she doesn't want to meet with me. She doesn't want to speak ill of the dead."

"There are a lot of people like that," Knox agreed. "Unfortunately, murder cases don't care about politeness."

"I'm not going to take no for an answer tomorrow," Ryan replied grimly. "I'm going to show up at her office and not leave until she talks to me. If she gives me a hard time, I'll call the detective on the case and they can bring her downtown. Perhaps she'll get the idea that we're not playing a game here."

They talked about Knox and Ryan meeting with Caroline, Danny, and Theo again. If anyone would know about Brad's gambling, it would be one of those.

"How about I order us some dinner?" Mariah offered. Ryan had had such a shit day she didn't want to ask him to fix a meal. And heaven knew she couldn't cook. She'd poison all three of them. "Pizza? Italian? Chinese? Burgers? There's a new sports bar that dropped off a menu a few weeks ago. There's cheese fries."

Ryan loved cheese fries. Or at least he had.

Knox placed his hand over his heart and sighed. "I would crawl over hot coals for a double cheeseburger. Do they have wings, too?"

"You bet."

She retrieved the menu from a drawer in the kitchen and

everyone put in their order, plus she said she'd add several items to share. They'd have leftovers, too.

"Do you guys mind if I go lie down while we wait for the food?" Knox asked, his hand on the doorknob. "I didn't sleep well on the flight."

"Go ahead," Ryan urged him. "Make yourself at home."

Knox was sleeping in the guest room of Ryan's apartment.

"He may have been tired but I think he also wanted to give us some time alone," Ryan said.

"He sounds like a good friend."

"He is. I'm lucky that all of my coworkers are good people."

"I'm going to call in the order," Mariah said. "Help yourself to another beer, if you want."

She put in their order, adding a few dishes that would make nice leftovers for the next day. By the time she was finished Ryan had left the living room. She looked in her bedroom, the guest room, and then finally found him in her studio space. He still had his beer in his hand and he was studying a painting she'd hung on the wall. It was a landscape of a spot in Central Park.

Their spot.

It had been a family vacation that was half business as well. Mariah had trailed along with the Becks because she was dating Ryan and best friends with Liza. It had been a lovely spring day and she and Ryan had gone for a walk through Central Park. At one spot there had been a beautiful flower garden and they'd stopped to look at it. Holding hands and kissing like the new lovers that they were, Ryan had told Mariah that he loved her.

She had, of course, happily said it back. It was one of her best memories of the past. The entire day had seemed so incredibly romantic. Like something out of a movie.

"I remember this place," he said.

"I have to admit that I still go back there whenever I visit New York. I still remember that day like it just happened."

He nodded, a smile playing on his lips. "You hung this one up. You didn't sell it."

"Because I don't normally paint landscapes, and I'm awful at it. It's not very good."

She didn't say that she'd never even tried to sell it. There's no way she could have.

"I think it's great," he said with a shake of his head. "But I'm glad you didn't sell it."

"I painted it for me."

"When did you paint it?"

He spoke so softly she almost didn't hear the question.

"Several years ago." She knew what he was really asking. "Before I got married to Bobby."

"Did you love him?"

She'd known that eventually they'd have this talk but she still wasn't quite prepared for it.

"Yes, but…"

She wasn't sure how to put it all into words.

"But…?"

"But not in the right way. I loved what he could have become, not who he was at the present. That's not a good basis for a marriage. I should have loved him for who he was."

"And he loved you."

"Yes, but I think he loved me in the same way that I loved him. He loved what he thought he could mold me into. He thought that after we got married that I'd change somehow. That I'd stop caring about my art and settle down and have a bunch of kids. He didn't like that I worked."

Bobby had wanted all of her attention on him. The truth was, he wanted *everyone's* attention on him and he didn't want to share the spotlight. When Mariah had received a writeup in an art magazine, he'd sulked for weeks.

Ryan frowned, his expression quizzical. "He didn't want you to paint? Why?"

"He wanted a more traditional wife," she explained. "I guess he thought I would change after the marriage vows. I thought he would change too, so I guess we're even. I shouldn't have married him. I see that now, but at the time…"

She didn't continue. Explaining it was only going to make her look even more stupid than she had actually been.

"I wanted to believe that love could change people," she finally said. "That it solved all problems. I should have known better."

"You didn't think I could change."

True. She hadn't and that was one of the reasons that they'd broken up. Somehow, she'd thought that Bobby could change. Maybe because he'd been older and supposedly more mature. It didn't make much sense looking back. She'd simply wanted to believe so badly because she wanted to be in love. She wanted her happily ever after. Now she knew it didn't work that way. Love wasn't handed out willy-nilly because you were a good person.

"Maybe...deep down...I thought I would change. But I didn't. And he didn't either. We didn't have a nasty divorce or anything. I think we both just realized that we made a mistake. The thing I truly regret is that I disappointed my parents. My mom had a little talk with me when Bobby and I got engaged. She tried to tell me that we were too different to make it work but I thought she was only saying that because she still wanted you to be my boyfriend."

That made Ryan smile.

"Your parents are the nicest, most wonderful people ever. I adore them."

"And they adore you," she said with a laugh. "You were the son they never had."

His smile instantly dropped. "And now? How are Mom and Dad going to feel about me possibly stealing their baby girl and taking her to Seattle? Are they going to hate me?"

"No, they'll just build a house near us and visit until we want to scream."

"Your parents could never make me scream."

"You say that now..."

His gaze shifted back to the painting, and she could see his shoulders tense.

"I've had a few somewhat serious relationships."

"I'm not sure what a somewhat serious relationship is," she replied carefully, not wanting to push back too hard. The fact was she curious. Liza had tried to keep Mariah in the loop about Ryan's romantic life, but she hadn't wanted to hear it. "Were you engaged?"

"No, but I thought about it once."

"Just once?"

Turning back to Mariah, he rubbed at his chin. "I was pretty focused on my career, to be honest, but there were a couple of women that I dated for awhile that I thought might turn into something. They didn't, obviously. They were good people. It just didn't work out."

"I'm kind of jealous," she admitted. "But I'm glad that you had someone in your life that made you happy. I wouldn't want to think about you being alone all the time."

"I'm kind of jealous, too."

It was a breathtaking admission from a man that didn't talk about his feelings much.

"We can't change the past, and I'm not sure that I would even if we could. I like the people that we became a hell of a lot more than the kids we were. We have a better chance this time. A real chance to make it work."

Reaching out, he pulled her in so their bodies were flush against one another. She slid her arms around his neck, her fingers playing with the curls at the nape of his neck, so soft and silky.

"I want to make this work, Mariah. I want that future with

you."

Together, they'd make it happen. It might be work, but it would be worth it.

CHAPTER TWENTY-FOUR

D INNER ARRIVED AND Knox came back to Mariah's apartment to eat. They all sat on the floor around the coffee table, talking about the day they'd had and their plans for tomorrow. The top of Ryan's list was a meeting with Isla. He wasn't going to take any more of her excuses.

"So what leads do you have left?" Mariah asked when they'd finished their meal. They'd all pitched in to clean up the mess, stuffing the leftovers into the refrigerator and the dirty plates and silverware into the dishwasher.

"Isla, Caroline, and Theo," Ryan replied as they all settled on the couch. "I'm hoping one of them knew about Brad's gambling."

"Caroline and Danny were quite forthcoming when you met with them," Mariah replied. "If she knew about it, I think she would have said something already."

"I've thought about that too, but I need to ask anyway. Maybe she didn't think it was an issue at the time."

"If anyone knows it will be his best buddy," Knox said. "Guys don't always tell their girls everything, but their best friend always knows the dirty details."

"Then why didn't Theo tell me when we talked before?" Ryan asked.

Knox grinned. "Bro code, dude. You don't rat on your best bro when they're doing something that others might not approve of."

"Even if Theo thought that Brad might be in over his head?"

"We don't have any evidence of that," Knox pointed out. "If he knew Brad was gambling, and I bet that he did, he may not have realized how much Brad was gambling a day. Or he may have known but didn't think it was a big deal since Brad's own daddy wasn't worried about the money. No alarm bells were going off anywhere and no one thought this was a problem."

That was the truth. Not one person had been concerned about Brad. Everyone said that he'd been acting normally. Nothing was off.

Then he'd walked into a bar and never walked out. Disappeared for over ten years. And he wasn't giving up his secrets easily either.

"I know I just got here," Knox continued. "But how about we start from the beginning? Go over the whole case again. That's what Jared would tell us to do."

Knox had worked for Jared as a deputy years ago.

Jason and Logan would have agreed with Jared, too.

"Okay, let's do that," Ryan agreed, levering up to grab a couple more beers from the refrigerator, but then he remembered that this wasn't his damn apartment and that Mariah might die of boredom listening to them talk shop. "We can go back to my place to do it. I don't want to take over your evening, Mariah."

"Are you kidding? I want to hear you two work. I promise I'll be as quiet as a mouse and just watch, but please stay here."

Ryan shook his head. "If we stay, I want you to speak up. You were there that night at the bar and you were also there when I talked to Caroline and Danny. You're in this as much as I am."

She looked unsure but Knox was nodding in agreement.

"He's right," Knox said. "You were there. You were Brad's friend. You have insights that I don't have."

"So you're unbiased," Mariah replied. "That's a really good thing."

"True," he agreed. "But we need all the brain power we can get here."

They gathered around the kitchen island, Ryan's case file spread out on the granite.

"So let's start at the beginning," he said. "We were all at the bar that night. The camera at the front door caught each one of us arriving and leaving. Except for Brad. The camera never shows him leaving. Yet, his body was found in the lot next door, so clearly he did exit the building."

"But not necessarily on his own power," Knox replied. "He may have been carried out at a later time."

Mariah grimaced. "You mean that he was hidden in that bar for some length of time? Ick."

"Sorry, gruesome shit doesn't gross me out anymore," Knox said. "But yes, that is what I'm saying. They could have hidden him in a crawl space, a basement, or even the attic. Then when the cameras were off or no one was there, they moved his body."

Ryan tapped his finger on one of the evidence photos – the one of the metal pipe that had been lying next to Brad's body. "But we know from the autopsy that Brad was likely killed by a blow to the head with this pipe. A pipe from the construction site next door. That has me leaning that he was alive and at the site."

"That site was under construction for months," Mariah said. "Anyone could have taken that pipe from there."

Ryan scratched at his chin. "They could have brought it inside but I'm still leaning toward him being attacked outside. Inside a crowded bar is no place for a deadly fight that no one will notice. And let's make it clear that no one noticed Brad having any issues with anyone that night."

Knox unfolded the police drawing of the construction site. "So we're saying that we think that Brad was alive when he exited the bar and that he was killed here? Because that begs the question of how the hell did he get out of the building without anyone seeing him? You said yourself that the back door has an alarm on it."

Mariah pointed to the west side of the bar on the drawing. "There were windows along here. It would have been a tight fit but he could have gotten out through one of them."

Ryan seized onto that detail. "According to the bar staff, he wasn't there after they pushed everyone out to close, and they checked the office and bathrooms each night in case some drunk decides they don't want to go home. So I think that makes the crawl through a window theory a probable one."

"We can try watching the video again," Knox suggested. "I can try enhancing it as much as possible. We need to be sure that he didn't exit out of the front door."

"It's old and terrible quality," Ryan warned him. "But it's worth a shot. At this point, we can't afford to ignore anything."

"I'll take a look at it," Knox promised. "If I can enhance it slightly, we might be able to get Jared to run some facial recognition software on it. Maybe we'll get a hit on someone who worked for a bookie."

The chance was small but they had to take it. They weren't rolling in leads at the moment.

"The only question is why did he do that?" Mariah asked quietly. "Why would he crawl out of a window instead of going out the front door? It doesn't make any sense."

"Because there was something or someone outside of the front door that he didn't want to see," Knox replied. "I'm guessing he owed someone money."

Mariah shook her head. "Brad's parents gave him plenty of money, especially after he started college. They weren't even worried about how much he was spending. He could have paid his debts."

"Maybe he placed a big bet," Ryan said. "A bet bigger than any he'd placed before and he lost. To pay it back, he might have had to take a bigger withdrawal than usual and he was worried about his parents finding out about his hobby."

She didn't look convinced.

"I guess that's a possibility, but I still don't see Brad not being able to pay for it. You said yourself he had plenty of money in the bank and a credit line, too. He also had control of the trust fund from his grandparents, remember? He got that when he turned twenty-one. Technically, he had millions."

"You have a valid point," Ryan conceded. "But I still agree with Knox that there had to be a damn good reason that Brad didn't go out the front door. Fear would be my only guess there. Maybe his fear didn't have anything to do with his gambling. It could be a red herring, and there was something else going on."

Knox rubbed the back of his neck and grimaced. "I don't want to speak ill of your friend, but you did say he was some-thing of a womanizer. Maybe he was running from a jealous boyfriend or husband. Hell, maybe he was just avoiding a woman that couldn't take a hint. I've been known to duck out of a bar when someone arrives that I was hoping not to see."

That was a distinct possibility. Ryan could picture a pissed-off boyfriend tracking down Brad to have it out.

"And that's the crux of this whole investigation, isn't it?" Mariah asked. "The reason Brad didn't go out the front door is probably the reason he ended up dead that night. But if we can't figure out the reason…"

She'd hit the nail on the head. Ryan believed that the reason Brad was dead was tied to why he didn't leave the bar the way the rest of them had that night. The big question was could he ever figure out what was going on?

"You've talked to all of Brad's friends and family," Knox said. "No one knew of anything strange going on."

"Except for Isla," Ryan said, his tone laced with frustration. "I haven't been able to talk to her."

"We'll definitely talk to her tomorrow," Knox promised. "Even if we have to have the cops bring her to the precinct. No more excuses."

"And Brad didn't show up at the airport or get on the plane," Mariah said. "Does that mean that we can assume that he never left the bar and construction site that night?"

Taking another sip of his now lukewarm beer, Ryan pondered that question. "We know he didn't get on the plane, and TSA didn't find any sign of him entering the airport when they investigated back then. Yes, I think we can say that it's likely that Brad didn't leave the area that night."

"This is good. What else can we say for sure?" Knox queried, pointing to the file. "We know that he was hit on the head, probably with that metal pipe found with his body. We know that the wound was on the side of his head, above his ear so there's a fifty-fifty chance that he was facing his attacker. We don't know if he had any defensive wounds because of the state of the body years later."

"We know that he was in touch with bookies," Ryan said. "We know that he spent a lot of money on women, partying, and booze. We also know that he had some struggles that semester in school but he pulled out good grades in the end."

"We know that he was cheating on Caroline," Mariah added. "We know that he was sleeping with Isla, and probably other women as well. We also know that Caroline was planning on ending it with Brad."

That was it. No one else spoke until eventually Knox broke the silence.

"Well…that's not a lot," he conceded. "But that's how these cold cases are. Nothing until you finally get a break. Let's hope that our talk with your friend Isla goes better tomorrow."

Mariah's phone buzzed with a call from her parents so she went into the bedroom to talk, leaving Ryan and Knox in the living room.

"I'm going to play Logan here," Knox said. "What's your gut telling you? That's what he'd ask."

Logan Wright's gut instincts were legendary. He'd caught a serial killer with them, after all.

Ryan didn't have to give it much thought. That was the point. Listen to his gut, not his brain.

"Not that my gut is anything like Logan's, but I'm kind of feeling like maybe the gambling isn't what got Brad killed. That there might be something else out there that we don't know. Mariah made an excellent point that Brad could find the money to pay his debts. Hell, he could have even come clean with his dad and Skip would have paid them. He was close with his parents and they wouldn't have let anything happen to him."

Knox nodded approvingly. "Mariah is a smart one. I'm leaning toward your theory as well. He had money to burn, basically, and while he might have been gambling big it doesn't seem like he was having any trouble from it. So then it has to be something else."

Something else. But what?

"Or a random tragedy," Knox added. "He may have pissed the wrong person off or been in the wrong place at the wrong time. It may have been completely unforeseen and nothing he brought on himself."

"Is that what you think?" Ryan asked. "The old chaos theory explanation?"

It wasn't out of the realm of possibility.

"Look at the crime. A hit to the head by a piece of metal that was probably lying on the ground near where they were standing. This isn't premeditated anything. This is a crime of passion or opportunity. A bookie's enforcer doesn't come to collect a debt but not bring his own weapon. That's not good planning. At least that's what my gut is telling me."

"I can't argue your logic."

"That leaves us one big open question, though," Knox replied.

"And that is?"

"Why in the fuck didn't your friend exit the bar through the goddamn front door? It doesn't make any sense."

The whole investigation was beginning to go in circles, all leading back to Brad having a fun evening with not a care in the world.

Until he was hit on the head with a pipe.

Ryan wasn't sure they'd ever know what truly happened that night, and he was afraid that this was one case he wasn't going to be able to solve.

CHAPTER TWENTY-FIVE

A T SOME POINT last night, it had been decided that Mariah would accompany Ryan and Knox when they talked to Caroline and Danny again. They'd gone back and forth but eventually felt that if Caroline became upset it would be good to have Mariah there to be a shoulder to lean on.

Mariah was fine with the decision and anxious to see Caroline again. Both she and Liza had made a vow to keep in touch with their friends from the past a bit better, and this was step one in that plan. She and Caroline had drifted apart, and they didn't have to be best friends who talked all the time, but they didn't have to be strangers either. There had to be a happy medium somewhere.

If Danny and Caroline thought it was strange that they were back to ask more questions, they were too polite to say so. As before, they were invited in and offered refreshments by the pool by the smiling couple. Knox was introduced and he made fast friends with the family dog. It was love at first sight between the two of them.

"I'm sorry that we have to bother you again," Ryan apologized when they were all settled around the table. It was a typically hot summer day so Danny had opened the large striped umbrella to shelter them from the sun. "But I have a few more questions that have come up during the investigation."

Danny put his arm around his wife's shoulders. "As we said before, we have no secrets. You can ask us anything you want."

Clearing his throat, Ryan took the lead on asking the questions. That had also been decided last night. Knox had said that he would stay mostly out of it, if possible. He was there for back up only if Ryan missed a follow-up question.

"During the investigation we've found that Brad was communicating with several bookies on a daily basis. Based on the amount of money he was withdrawing and depositing in his account, we think he was heavily involved in gambling. We were wondering if you were aware of this."

Caroline's eyes had gone wide and even the usual unflappable Danny looked shocked.

"Gambling?" she repeated. "Are you saying he was addicted to gambling? Because I know that he placed bets from time to time. He'd tell me about them. I never thought it was a big deal."

"You think this is what got him killed?" Danny asked, before anyone could answer his wife. "That he owed money and they murdered him?"

Ryan shook his head. "Not necessarily. It's simply one avenue that we're looking at. Did either of you see Brad worried about finances at all?"

"Brad was never worried about money," Caroline replied firmly. "Ever. He never worried about what anything cost or where the money would come from. I never saw him concerned about it in the least."

That would have been Mariah's response as well. Brad wasn't a person who worried about much of anything, especially money. And for good reason; he didn't have the worries that average people did.

"Me neither," Danny agreed. "I don't ever remember Brad worried about much of anything except his grades that last semester. He said that if he didn't fix them then his mom and dad would be disappointed. That's it. That's all that I ever remember him being concerned about."

"Did Brad have any new friends during that time?" Knox asked, giving the dog a scratch behind the ears. "Did he use any new names that you weren't familiar with?"

Danny shook his head, but Caroline nodded. "Actually, he did. We were out at a movie the night after he got back to Chicago. His phone was off during the film but afterward he checked his messages and he said that he needed to return Aaron's call. I have no clue who Aaron was, and I think that I said that, but I don't remember him answering me. He just said that he was going to call him back and told me to go ahead inside of the restaurant and order for both of us. I did and when he came back he didn't say anything about the call. I guess I just assumed that he was a friend from college."

"Aaron," Ryan repeated. "No last name?"

"No last name," Caroline confirmed. "He only mentioned him that one time. That's why I didn't think it was important."

It wasn't much to go on in Mariah's eyes. If Ryan and Knox could find out anything about some mysterious guy from over ten years ago with no last name that would be amazing.

They chatted a little bit more but Caroline and Danny didn't have anything else to add. Brad hadn't been acting strangely and he didn't seem worried about anything.

Mariah gave her friend a hug when they all stood up to leave. "Liza and I are going to call you and take you out to lunch soon. If you want to, that is."

Caroline smiled and hugged back. "I'd like nothing more. If you don't call me, I'm going to call you."

Danny walked them to the front door. "So I guess we'll see you at the party tonight. Caroline and I are excited to have an evening out of the house without the kids."

Mariah hadn't even realized that Caroline and Danny were invited, which when she thought about it was kind of stupid. Of course, Liza would have invited them and their parents, too. All their families had been friends for years. That's why their generation had ended up together.

"It's going to be a great party," Ryan remarked. "Liza has party planning down to an art."

She did, and it would be.

Danny's smile fell and he hesitated for a moment. "There's not going to be clowns there, right? Like at your twenty-first?"

Liza had gone behind Ryan's back and ordered a couple of

clowns for his twenty-first birthday party. Ryan *hated* clowns, and Mariah wasn't all that fond of them either. They were a little creepy in her opinion but she realized that some people loved them. She just wasn't one of them.

Anyway, it had been a prank between brother and sister, but it turned out that several people at the party didn't like clowns so Ryan had ordered them to leave, telling them that they'd get paid either way. They'd exited the venue immediately.

"No clowns," Ryan assured Danny. "Mom wasn't happy about that and it's her birthday. I think Liza has learned her lesson."

"It's pink-themed," Mariah said when the three of them were in her car and driving away. "You know...everything is pink. The tablecloths, the champagne, twinkle lights, the cake. She said your mother loves pink."

"My mother does love pink," Ryan replied. "I hope she loves it when everything around her looks like a five-year-old's room exploded."

"I don't think Liza chose a pink that bright. She used the words soft and classic."

"I'm just grateful that she didn't ask all of us to wear pink. That's where I draw the line."

Knox laughed. "Aw, come on. A pink bow tie and a matching pocket square. That could be tasteful. Do you think it's too girly?"

"I'm secure enough to wear pink," Ryan chuckled. "I just don't think it's my color."

Mariah had to ask. She'd been thinking about since Caroline had mentioned it.

"So does what Caroline told you about this guy named Aaron help? Can you do anything with that?"

"We can," Knox replied confidently. "It won't be easy, but if we dig deep we might find something. I'll go back through Brad's phone records and see if any of the numbers belong to an Aaron. We'll also go back through his credit card statements and emails."

"It might not be helpful though," Ryan. "Aaron may just be someone that Brad met at school. He may not have anything to do with what happened to him that night."

"But it's a lead?" Mariah pressed. "It might be helpful?"

"It might," Ryan agreed. "We have to follow every available trail until we've exhausted them all."

"Then we start all over again," Knox added. "We don't give up until there's literally nothing left to go on. We still have leads to follow. Your friend Isla might know something. She's been ducking Ryan's calls and that's sort of suspicious to me."

"She's not going to duck me any longer," Ryan said grimly. "That's where I'm going next. I'm going to talk to her whether she likes it or not."

When Ryan Beck was determined to do something, no one was going to stop him.

KNOX WENT TO meet with Theo while Ryan headed to Isla's day

spa just outside of Chicago in one of the well-to-do suburbs. She had a whole string of day spas but one call to the downtown location and he was able to find out which one she was at today. It hadn't even been difficult. They'd easily offered him the information. He should have done this two days ago instead of calling Isla directly and leaving messages. He'd thought he was being polite and understanding for an old friend but now he was simply annoyed.

The waiting room of the day spa had a tinkling waterfall on one wall, soft carpet, deep leather couches, and the scent of some sort of potpourri or candle hung in the air. Maybe jasmine? He wasn't an expert. The woman behind the counter welcomed him with a big smile and a soft voice. There was a sign on the wall asking people to silence their phones.

This was a quiet, stress-free zone, apparently.

"I need to speak to Isla Norton."

The woman frowned and glanced at her computer screen. "Do you have an appointment? She's very busy."

He'd had enough of Isla's runaround. It wasn't this person's fault, but he wasn't going to be shown to the door.

"So am I. I'm an old friend of Isla's and she knows why I'm here. She can either talk to me right now or I can have the police come down here and escort her to the station. You can tell her it's her choice. I'll wait while you do that."

And then he did just that, declining to take a seat when it was offered. He stood at the counter while the obviously flustered woman hurried through a side door while the other patrons gave him curious looks. It was only a moment later when she stepped out of that doorway and addressed him.

"Isla will see you now."

"Thank you."

The woman gave him a scowl as he walked past, letting him know in no uncertain terms she found him to be a rude asshole.

She's not the first. Definitely won't be the last.

Isla's office was as opulent as her waiting room, with a large glass desk positioned in front of a picture window. There was another leather couch against the wall and a second waterfall to Ryan's left. Even the carpet seemed design to muffle any steps or noise.

"Ryan! It's so good to see you."

Isla gave him a hug, all smiles and welcome which surprised him. He'd assumed she would be angry at the way he'd butted into her office.

"It's good to finally see you too, Isla. I've been trying to talk to you for a couple of days now."

She threw up her hands and laughed. "I've been so busy lately. We're expanding to a new location and I swear I have nothing but meetings all day."

He had to tamp down the annoyance that immediately rose at her seemingly careless attitude. He needed her cooperation.

"I've been trying to talk to you about Brad," Ryan said. "I'm investigating his murder, as you know."

"I do know," she said, waving her arm toward the couch. "Let's sit down and catch up."

Ryan didn't want to *catch up* with Isla, he wanted answers to his questions.

"We need to talk about Brad. Why haven't you returned my calls?"

Her eyes widened and she appeared shocked at his frustrated tone. "I got your messages but I didn't think it was all that important."

Christ on a crutch, had Isla always been like this?

Yes, she had. He was now remembering how difficult she'd always been. And not for any particular reason, just because she liked to be in control and have her way.

"You didn't think a murder investigation was important? What would be important in your eyes, Isla?"

She pursed her lips and shrugged. "Brad's been gone a long time. What's a few more days?"

"Your empathy is overwhelming. I take it you didn't like Brad that much."

Hopping up from the couch, Isla shook her finger at Ryan. "I liked Brad. He was a nice guy. I liked the real him, the person you all didn't even know. But he's been gone for a long time and does it really matter how it all happened? It won't bring him back."

As usual, Isla wasn't thinking about anyone but herself.

"It matters to his family. Just because it doesn't matter to you doesn't mean that everyone thinks like you do."

"It won't bring him back," she repeated, her chin lifted. "Besides, I don't see how I can help your investigation. I don't know what happened to Brad that night. I left the bar and never saw him again."

"But you were seeing him," Ryan stated. "Everyone knows you were sleeping with Brad."

Rolling her eyes, she grabbed a water bottle from her desk and took a drink before replying. "Yes, we were sleeping together. That doesn't mean I know what happened to him that night. We weren't a couple. We were fucking."

"That means that you were spending time with Brad those last weeks before he disappeared. We know that he was in contact with multiple bookies and he was spending tens of thousands of dollars. Did you know he had a gambling problem? Was he upset or worried about anything? Did he mention anyone new? Perhaps an Aaron?"

He didn't mean to throw out all of his questions at once, but he was trying to get Isla to realize that this wasn't a social call. This was a serious murder investigation.

Her brows pinched together, she shook her head. "Brad was not addicted to gambling. Yes, he gambled but he wasn't addicted."

"The number of calls he made on a daily basis tells a different story."

She shook her head again. "It doesn't make any sense. He placed a few bets here and there but he wasn't addicted."

"You sound sure."

"I'm not completely, absolutely sure, but Brad didn't have an addictive personality," she argued, her arms crossed over her chest. "He was actually surprisingly mature once you got past all of that macho fraternity bro bullshit. He was a sensitive guy deep down, but he didn't want anyone to know. He thought it made him look weak."

"But he didn't mind showing you?"

Ryan wasn't sure Isla was being honest with him. He wouldn't have cared if Brad wasn't a hard-partying asshole.

"He knew that he could be himself with me and that I wouldn't judge him. He could just explore who he was and who he wanted to be and it would be okay."

"Sounds like you two had a hell of a three weeks together."

Isla smiled and softly laughed. "Brad and I had been sleeping together for about three years, Ryan. We didn't talk about it because it was nobody's fucking business but ours. So yes, you could say that I knew Brad well. I certainly knew him a hell of a lot better than Caroline ever did. She was in love with a fantasy. He was never going to marry her."

"Was he going to marry you?"

"I hope not. I wasn't in love with him, and I don't think he was in love with me either. We…accepted each other, for want of a better description. In fact, because we didn't love each other it made it easier for Brad to be himself."

In a weird, twisted way it made sense.

"And that included multiple partner sex?"

Giggling, she nodded. "My goodness, you have done your homework, Ryan. I'm impressed. It's true. Brad liked to explore his sexual boundaries and I was happy to help him. It's not against the law."

"And you're saying that you knew the real Brad?"

"I'm only saying that there was more to him than the facade that he let others see."

Ryan had never seen any glimmer of the person she was describing, but then he and Brad hadn't been close for a few years before his death. It wasn't out of the realm of possibility that Brad had finally grown up.

"Good, then you can tell me if he was worried or concerned about anything before his disappearance. Money? Friends? School?"

"He was never worried about money or school," she replied with a shake of her head. "The only thing he ever worried about was his family. He was very concerned about them. They were kind of dysfunctional."

His family?

"What about his family had him worried?"

"His parents' marriage was bad. I guess they would argue so loudly the whole house would hear. His mother would throw things at his dad, and then his dad would drive off and not come back for days. And then the whole thing with his little brother. Brad was worried that Seb was growing up too fast. He hated that Seb was around his parents when they were fighting."

Ryan hadn't known that at all but every family had their secrets. It sounded like the Harringtons might have a few ugly ones.

"One more question. Did you ever hear the name Aaron?"

"No, should I have heard it?"

"I don't know. Caroline said that Brad took a call from someone named Aaron a few days before he disappeared."

"I never heard Brad talk about anyone named Aaron. Sorry, I can't help you there." There was an impatient knock at the door. "Are we done here? I have another meeting."

"We're done. Thanks for talking to me."

"You didn't need to threaten me with the police. I would have talked to you today."

She looked slightly pissed off.

"Then next time return your messages when someone is calling you about a murder."

"That's the problem with you, Ryan. You've always been too dramatic, too serious."

I don't think that's my problem.

"I'll take that opinion under consideration."

Isla threw back her head and laughed. "Which means you're saying *fuck you* in your head. I know you, Ryan Beck, and you don't give a shit about my opinions."

"That's true, but you don't care about mine either. I guess we're even."

"I guess we are. It was still good to see you. Say hi to Mariah for me."

"I will. It was nice to see you, too."

"You're such a terrible liar." She walked with him to the office door. "Seriously, do you think you'll find out what happened to Brad that night?"

"I'm trying. It won't be easy all these years later."

Although now he had a new avenue to look down thanks to Isla – Brad's dysfunctional family. There had been rumors years ago that Skip had been having an affair, and that Lilly was spending far too much time with her tennis pro. What else might be going on behind the curtain?

"What do you think happened to Brad?" he asked, his hand on the doorknob. "Do you have a theory?"

She didn't answer for a long moment, her gaze far away. "For a long time, I told myself that he just went off and started a new life. But I knew deep down he would never do that. He was devoted to his family. Eventually, I assumed that he'd been in the wrong place at the wrong time. He was probably mugged or got in a fight with someone who didn't have much left to lose. So that's what I think happened. If he had gone home with Caro or Theo that night, he'd probably be alive today."

Ryan bid Isla goodbye and headed back to the apartment to get ready for his mother's birthday party. It looked like he had more questions for Skip, Lilly, and Seb.

They hadn't been telling him the whole truth.

CHAPTER TWENTY-SIX

"**Y**OU GO AHEAD to the party," Ryan said, tapping away at the keyboard of his laptop. "I'll catch up to you in an hour or so. I really need to finish this."

Mariah exchanged a glance with Knox. Ryan had told her that he had apologized to his dad and that everything was better than ever with his parents, but now he was making an excuse not to go to the birthday party.

Knox just shrugged and stepped away so Mariah could talk to Ryan alone.

"You cannot skip your mother's birthday party. You'll hurt her terribly and Liza will be livid."

He looked up from the laptop. "I'm not skipping the party. I just need to do this research into the Harrington family. I'm pissed off at myself for not doing it in the first place, but I was just so focused on all of us at the bar that night. I'll be right behind you, just a little late. That's all."

"Doesn't your boss Jared usually do the computer research?"

"He does, but he's busy tonight."

"What about Knox?"

The other man must have heard his name even though he was on the other side of the room.

"I can do it, Ryan. You go ahead to the party. Your parents don't care if I'm there."

Liza had insisted that Knox join them tonight, and Ryan had even lent him a tuxedo from his Chicago closet. Knox had expressed his fascination that a person could own more than one tux. He'd joked that he was strictly a renter of formal wear.

"I'm really close to finishing. Just go ahead," Ryan insisted. "I swear I'll be right behind you. If I handed this to you, you'd just have to start over."

Mariah wasn't quite sure what to do. If she showed up at the party without Ryan she was going to get shit from Liza. But she knew Ryan well, and he wasn't going to budge here. He was in the zone, so to speak, and barely noticing that other people existed.

So much for my new dress and all the time I took with my hair and makeup.

"Fine," she finally said. "But if you're not there in an hour, I'm getting in the car and forcibly removing you from that chair and dragging you to the party."

"And I'll help her," Knox declared with a grin. "One hour, bro."

"One hour," Ryan agreed, not even looking up from the screen. "I promise. I don't want to upset my mother either. I'll be there. I'm already dressed. I just need to put my jacket and shoes on."

There wasn't anything left to argue about. Mariah dropped her lipstick and keys into her tiny handbag and checked her makeup in the mirror next to the door while Knox leaned down to whisper something into Ryan's ear. She didn't know what he said, but Ryan stopped what he was doing and stood up, striding over to where she was standing.

"Before you go, I just wanted to tell how goddamn gorgeous you look tonight, babe," Ryan said, enfolding her into his strong arms. "I'm not going to kiss you because I don't want to mess up your lipstick but you're going to turn every single head tonight. You're absolutely beautiful."

Mariah looked up at the man she loved. He was so full of it sometimes.

"Knox told you to come over and say that didn't he?"

She loved him, but she wasn't stupid either. Ryan had been heads down and not paying a damn bit of attention to the slinky purple and silver evening gown she was wearing. She'd loved it the moment she'd put it on, although the plunging back had been a bit more daring than she usually went for. She'd paired it with silver high heeled sandals and a simple clip holding back one side of her long hair behind her ear.

"He told me that you were leaving and that I needed to get my head out of my ass."

"I'll take that as a yes."

"I already knew you were a knockout," he said with a smile. "I just forget to tell you. It won't happen again."

It probably would, but that was fine. He was going to get

lost in his work, and frankly, so was she.

"I don't need compliments to turn my head. I just need you."

"You got me, baby," he declared, waggling his eyebrows. "Now brace yourself because I'm about to mess up your lipstick."

He did just that, thoroughly kissing her until she was breathless. The ever-thoughtful Knox had taken himself out in the hallway between the two apartments to give them privacy, which she thought was very sweet.

"One hour," she reminded him, freshening her smeared lipstick. It had been totally worth it, though. "Then I send out a posse. Dead or alive, you're coming to that party."

"I'll be there. Leave me some food at the buffet."

"You snooze, you lose. I make no promises."

With a wave she exited the apartment, leaving Ryan to his work. The car service had just pulled up to the curb and before she knew it, she and Knox were on their way to the party.

"I'm glad you're coming tonight," she said as the city lights whisked past them. The Chicago skyline was beautiful. She loved this city and would be sad to leave, but she was determined that this time she and Ryan were going to do it right. If she needed to move, then that's what she'd do. "I think you'll have a good time. Beck parties are always fun."

"I don't know much about fancy parties. My family usually just grilled some burgers and hot dogs in the backyard. The last time I wore a tux was when I was best man in my buddy's wedding. I just hope I don't do anything impolite like use the wrong fork or use the napkins as a bib."

The image of Knox wearing a bib had her laughing.

"You'll be fine. It's a buffet so there's no sit-down dinner. A lot more relaxed. And if you want to wear your napkin as a bib, I say go for it. It might help some of these stodgy people relax a little bit."

"I don't think I want to draw attention to myself. I'm happy to stand in the corner and eat the shrimp."

"I don't think you're going to get that lucky," she scoffed. "As handsome as you are, you're going to get a great deal of attention from the single women. Some of the married ones, too. You're going to be in big demand tonight. Can you dance?"

"Let's just say I can get by if it's not too complicated."

"Then you're really going to be popular. You won't get a moment of peace all night."

Chuckling, he gave her a cocky grin. "That sounds like my idea of the perfect evening."

Mariah had a strong feeling that Knox didn't have any trouble with the opposite sex.

"I'm glad you're here for Ryan," she said after a few quiet minutes. "I can't help him with this investigation, and I know he's frustrated."

"It's personal for him," Knox replied. "So it's going to mean more. But it's personal for you too, right? You were friends with Brad as well."

"I was but not as close as Ryan was, although to be fair we'd both pulled back from Brad a bit. He was closer to Danny and Theo."

Knox had spoken with Theo earlier that day and he didn't know anything about Brad having a gambling problem. He was quite dubious about the entire situation, saying that Brad never showed signs of it.

"I would imagine as you and Ryan got more serious, you didn't hang out with your friend group as much. Not that I've been that serious," he said with a laugh. "But I've seen it with other people. It's normal, I think."

"We were pretty serious, but we ended up apart. I think we both needed to grow up."

"From what I've seen Ryan is pretty damn adult. Scarily responsible."

"That's good news," Mariah laughed. "I hope I've grown up a little, too."

"I think you both are going to do fine. You've got to believe."

"That's good advice, Knox. Have you ever thought about becoming a relationship counselor?"

Knox threw back his head and laughed. "Fuck, no. I don't know shit about relationships. But I do know when two people can't take their eyes off of one another. That's you and Ryan. I have a feeling I'll be seeing you in Seattle before too long."

Seattle. Chicago. Did it matter where in the world they were?

As long as she was with Ryan, she was at home.

★ ★ ★

FIFTY MINUTES AND counting. Ryan had ten more minutes to get here or Mariah was going to go back to the apartment and drag him out. Her fingers itched to grab her phone and give him a call, but then she'd stop. She had to trust that he'd show. He wasn't the stubborn, always right-never wrong man that she'd dated years ago. He wouldn't break his word, and he wouldn't hurt his mother.

In the meantime, Mariah had posted herself close to the buffet and had already eaten through one plate of food and was contemplating a second trip. There was a carving station that she hadn't visited yet and the roast beef looked delicious.

I definitely need to have some of that. But I need to save room for cake, too.

As predicted, Knox was the hit of the party with any female under the age of eighty. He was a charmer, for sure, and flirted with everyone. At first, he'd tried to stick close to her, but she'd happily waved him off to the dance floor. She'd whispered in his ear that she'd be fine and to go have fun. These were people she'd known her whole life so she felt extremely comfortable without a date.

"If my brother doesn't show up tonight, I'm going to kill him," Liza declared, sidling up next to Mariah. "And I'll enjoy every single minute of it, too."

"You'll have to wait in line because he swore up and down that he'd be here."

"He'd better. Mom and Dad have already asked about him."

"He'll be here." Mariah smiled as she remembered Knox's words in the car. "You have to believe."

"Mariah, where is Ryan?" Skip Harrington asked, entering the dining room. Ryan's dad Jack was with him. "I haven't seen him tonight."

"He had some work to do but he should be here any minute."

"That's my boy," Jack said with a smile. "Nose to the grindstone. He was always that way even when he was a kid."

"A good hard worker," Skip said with a nod. "Ambitious and motivated."

"Where's Seb?" Mariah queried, her gaze running over the room. "I hope he and his wife were able to make it tonight."

She'd already greeted Lilly earlier when they both on the verandah getting some fresh air.

"I'm not sure," Skip replied. "He's around here somewhere. Maybe he's outside."

"I didn't see him arrive," Liza said. "And I thought I'd greeted all the guests personally."

"He was a little late," Skip said. "But he's definitely here. Sandy, too. They might be dancing."

"They're definitely not dancing,"

That statement came from a deep voice behind Mariah.

Ryan. He'd made it in less than an hour. Just as he'd promised.

"Then they're probably outside," Skip said. "This is a big house and grounds. They could be anywhere."

"I really need to talk to Seb," Ryan pressed. He had a strange, intense look on his face and he'd barely acknowledged Mariah. His attention was firmly on Skip. "Can you send him a text and ask him to meet me here in the dining room? It's important."

Something flickered across Skip's expression that Mariah couldn't quite identify. Fear? Anger? Perhaps something else. Either way, Skip didn't look too happy.

"It's a party, Ryan. Can it wait?" Jack asked. "You can talk to Seb tomorrow."

"No, I need to talk to him tonight. It's important. It's about the investigation."

There was an awkward silence between them as the party went on around them. Ryan didn't waver for a moment, his gaze never leaving Skip. Jack kept looking between his son and best friend, frowning the whole time. It looked like he wanted to say something but wasn't sure how to break the wall of tension.

"How about I go look for Seb?" Liza offered in an overly cheerful tone. "I'll find him and bring him here."

"That's a great idea," Ryan said, finally turning his gaze away from Skip. "I'll look for him, too. Between the two of us, we'll find him."

Mariah opened her mouth to offer to help but never got the chance. Before she could get a word out Skip had grabbed her roughly by the arm, dragging her in front of him. A human shield between him and Ryan.

Holy shit, had Skip Harrington murdered his own son?

Am I next?

CHAPTER TWENTY-SEVEN

I T WAS DEAD silent in the dining room. Ryan could hear the air conditioning kick on, the cool air floating on the back of his now damp neck.

It took everything inside of him to outwardly act calm. Inside, he was screaming like an animal battering at the iron bars of a cage but he sure as fuck didn't want Skip Harrington to know that. He didn't want the older man to think that he was perturbed in the least.

Especially when Skip had a knife from the nearby carving station to Mariah's vulnerable neck.

"I won't let you hurt her. Just put the knife down, Skip. We can work this out."

Not once during the drive to Ryan's parents' home had he thought that Skip had killed his own son. Now it looked like the older man had a great deal to hide.

Skip shook his head and pressed the knife more firmly against Mariah's vulnerable flesh.

"We don't need to work this out. I just need to keep you here long enough for Seb to get out of the country."

Seb? The pieces were beginning to fall into place.

Taking a few breaths before he replied, Ryan tried to steady himself. His emotions were all over the place, his instincts screaming to run over and knock Skip away from Mariah. His overriding concern had to be getting her – and everyone else here – safely away from the older man.

Mariah, to her credit, hadn't lost her shit despite having a knife to her throat. Her chest rose and fell rapidly and if he could hear her heartbeat he was sure it would be galloping as fast as his own, but she hadn't said a word. She'd barely moved, clearly deciding that she was going to stay still so as not to upset Skip Harrington.

It was a wise move on her part. He hoped he was giving her an encouraging look but he didn't have a clue as to how he was coming across. Normally, he'd be logical and cool in a situation like this. But Skip Harrington knew exactly what to do to keep Ryan off balance...

"Why does Seb need to get out of the country?" Ryan asked, keeping his tone even and soft. "Did he hurt Brad?"

Skip took a step back, pulling Mariah with him, his expression pale and tortured.

"It was an accident. He didn't mean anything bad to happen. It was just a terrible accident," Skip said, his voice hoarse with emotion.

"I believe you. You need to give Seb an opportunity to explain that," Ryan said. "He won't go to jail if it was an accident."

"I can't take that chance," Skip replied with a shake of his head. His hand tightened on the knife, and even from Ryan's vantage point he could see the knuckles turn white. "I won't lose my only remaining son. I won't let anything happen to him. I have to protect him. They just got into a fight and things got out of hand."

"Of course you have to protect him, but this isn't the way," Ryan argued, taking a tiny step forward. Small enough that he hoped it wouldn't spook the older man. "Let Seb tell his story."

There was a visible sheen of sweat on Mariah's forehead and upper lip. She'd held herself together for this long, but Ryan couldn't guarantee that she was going to be able to continue. He had to get her away from Skip.

"Just let Mariah go," Ryan cajoled, his tone calm even as his guts churned inside of him. Fear clawed at his abdomen and he had to fight his urge to use physical force to separate Skip and Mariah. That could have a tragic ending he didn't want to think about. He just hoped that Skip wouldn't actually hurt anyone. He was desperate at the moment and needed to be convinced that this wasn't how to help his son. "Let her go and we'll talk."

"You'll call the police and they'll stop him from flying out of the country," Skip argued. "Once he gets on that plane and it takes off, I'll let her go."

"It's going to make him look guilty," Ryan said. "People will say that he did something wrong."

"Let them say that. He'll be free and I'll have my son. I'll protect him no matter what."

Ryan was just about to reply when his father Jack stepped

forward, his own hands held up in a sign of surrender.

"It was an accident, old friend. Just tell the police and they'll understand. Seb won't go to jail. Let Mariah go and we'll do it together," Jack said. Ryan could hear the pain in his own father's voice. "What you're doing is wrong and you know it."

"He's my only son now," Skip said, his voice quivering. He was beginning to look tired, drops of sweat on his forehead and his eyes turning glassy. This might be the opening that Ryan was looking for. He just had to be patient. "I have to protect him."

Jack shook his head, his expression sad. "At some point we have to stop trying to protect our sons and just hope that we did a good job as parents. And we did a good job, Skip. Our sons are fine men. But we can't live their lives for them. We can't make their decisions for them, and we sure as hell can't stop them from facing the consequences of their actions. We have to let go."

Tears began to fall down Skip's face but his grip tightened on the knife. "What if they take him away? I can't lose another son."

"You have to let Seb stand up for himself," Jack pressed. "We can't make everything okay for our kids no matter how much we want to. Let Mariah go, Skip. You know you're not really going to hurt her. You could never do that."

Out of the corner of Ryan's eye, he could see Knox entering the dining room behind Skip. He'd been patient but it was time to take a chance. Ryan let his gaze dart to the left of Skip, just over his shoulder. Holding this breath, he hoped that the older man would wonder what Ryan was looking at.

It worked.

Skip, for only a moment, slackened his hold on Mariah as he jerked his head to the right, allowing the hand that held the knife to drop a few inches.

That was the opening that Ryan needed. Roaring with fury, he rushed Skip, grabbing his wrist and wrenching his arm away while pushing Mariah to safety. He trusted that Knox would keep her safe while he dealt with the other man.

Knocking Skip to the floor, he held him down while the man fought and howled but it didn't last long. He gave up, tears streaming down his cheeks, lying on the maple hardwood flooring. Ryan stepped back and his father took his place, kneeling next to his friend.

Knox had, indeed, done as Ryan hoped, placing his body between Mariah and Skip.

"Don't hurt Seb," Skip sobbed, his face red and swollen. "Just let him go. He didn't mean to do it."

His pulse still racing, Ryan stood and walked on shaking legs to where Mariah was watching the entire scene with a look of horror on her face. He doubted she was used to dealing with murders in the family.

"Are you okay?" he whispered, cradling her ashen cheeks in his hands. Her beautiful eyes were shiny with emotion and her lips trembling visibly. "Should we call a doctor?"

"I'm okay. Just shaken up." She glanced down at where Skip was lying on the floor. His wife Lilly had joined Jack in trying to talk to him and get him to stand up. "I don't think he really would have hurt me."

"Let's just be glad we didn't have to find that out."

It was then that Ryan noticed that the entire party had come to a halt and everyone was standing around them in a circle...staring.

"Show's over, folks," Knox said, beginning to usher some of the guests out of the dining room. "If you could please exit, that would be helpful."

Ryan reached for his cell phone in his breast pocket. "We need to call–"

"Done it," Knox replied. "The police should be here any minute. I also told them that Seb Harrington was probably on a charter jet out of the country. They're going to try and see if they can stop the takeoff, but I guess there are several airstrips that he could be flying out of. I couldn't be more helpful about that."

Grimacing, Ryan's father also stood. "Call them back and tell them to try the Carlisle private airstrip. That's the one that Skip uses most often."

Knox's brows rose. "Will do. I'll call them now. Thank you."

Jack turned to Ryan and placed a hand on his shoulder. "You did a good job, son."

Glancing toward Skip and Lilly, Ryan wasn't so damn sure. "Your best friend's son accidentally killed his brother, and that best friend is trying to cover it up. I'm not sure that I did such a great job."

"You did your job," Jack replied, his expression solemn.

"You're not responsible for how this turned out."

That may have been true, but Ryan didn't feel the usual elation or the satisfaction of an investigation closed. The situation was messed up and a lot of lives had been ruined today.

"How did you know?" Mariah asked. "How did you know it was Seb?"

"I didn't," Ryan immediately answered. "I actually just wanted to talk to him because my research showed that Seb had gone into rehab a few months after Brad disappeared. The rehab center not only dealt in drug addictions but also gambling addictions. At that point, I realized that Brad must have been covering for his little brother and may have been killed in a case of mistaken identity. Seb and Brad looked a hell of a lot alike and it seemed plausible. I didn't realize Seb was the one until Skip mentioned him."

"I thought it was Skip," she said, placing her arm into his and leaning into him. He wrapped his arms around her, needing to feel her healthy and alive. For a moment, he'd had to face the thought of losing her. He never wanted to do that again. "When he grabbed me I just assumed it was him. I was shocked."

"I would never have let him hurt you. You know that, right?"

His gaze searched hers, wanting her to know the truth and what he saw almost brought him to his knees. His heart squeezed in his chest and he had to make himself breathe in and out because oxygen simply wasn't all that important at this moment.

"I know," she said, love and trust shining from her eyes. "I knew you'd figure it all out and you did."

"I love you."

The words came out choked but he couldn't have meant them more than if he'd hired a skywriter to write the words over the Greater Chicago area.

"I love you, too."

He didn't really give a shit that there were people watching and sirens in the background. He kissed her until he heard his dad clearing his throat over and over and his sister tugging on his jacket sleeve.

"Not here, big brother. Later."

"This is all your fault," Mariah said smugly to Liza. "If you hadn't convinced me to buy the apartment across from Ryan's..."

"I would have sought you out and found you," Ryan said. "Because I couldn't stay away from you. End of story."

He dropped a kiss on the tip of Mariah's nose. "I have to get back to work."

"I'll be here. Take your time."

The thought of coming home to Mariah every night after a long day of work was...

Perfect. Amazing. Fantastic.

He didn't have the adjectives to describe all that he was feeling, but he had a future with this woman, and suddenly that was all he wanted in his life.

She was everything and more. And she loved him back.

CHAPTER TWENTY-EIGHT

Six months later...

MARIAH WATCHED AS Ryan and his friends carried in a stack of pizza boxes and several six packs of beer, water, and soda. The movers had just dropped off her boxes and they'd all offered to help pitch in and unpack for the measly compensation of pizza and a few cold beverages.

I'd take that deal any day.

She'd officially moved to the Seattle area. She and Ryan had gone back and forth about whether he would move to Chicago or she would move here, but the bottom-line was that his job was here and she could work anywhere. That he'd promised to buy her a home with an amazing studio space was the icing on the cake. He'd been true to his word, too. They'd closed on the house last week.

Now they were making plans to merge their two Chicago apartments into one big one for when they visited their families. They were going to need the space.

Mariah was pregnant. Twelve weeks along.

They probably should have waited longer but once they were

together and making plans for their future, they couldn't really see a reason to delay. In their minds, they'd already waited twelve years. They hadn't been in a hurry, either, but they'd somehow managed it the first month they'd tried. She hoped it boded well for the future as they'd discussed having at least two and maybe three kids.

They'd told their families a few days ago and Ryan wanted to tell his friends today. He'd been bouncing around like a Labrador puppy all morning, grinning from ear to ear. His friends didn't know what was going on but they'd been teasing him about love making him giddy since they'd arrived.

They chatted while demolishing several large pizzas. Mariah had been lucky and hadn't experienced any morning sickness so she ate her share. When everyone was done eating, he gave her a wink and stood, holding up his glass.

"I'd like to make a toast," he said. "To my soon to be wife, Mariah. I love you more than anything in the world and I can't wait for our baby to be born in six months."

Pandemonium. Hugs, tears, and congratulations.

Mariah had grown close to Ryan's friends and their significant others, although Knox would always have a special place in her heart.

When a guy puts his body between you and a knife, you know he's a good person.

"We didn't even know you were trying," Ella said, her hand on her own baby bump. She was married to Ryan's co-worker Chris Marks and due in about a month. They already had a daughter from Chris's first marriage who was adorable and incredibly intelligent. Annalise was going to rule the world someday. "It's so exciting. Do you want a boy or a girl?"

"It doesn't matter to me," Mariah replied. "Ryan might want a boy, though."

He shook his head. "Doesn't matter to me either. I just want them to be healthy and happy."

Luke reached over and grabbed his fiancée Shaw's hand. "What do you say, babe? Should we start trying right away?"

Shaw rolled her eyes. "That would be a no, handsome. We still have to get through our wedding in the summer. Then we can talk about it. How about you two? Are you moving the date up?"

Mariah shook her head. "We talked about it but the plans are set for next year and I don't want to mess with them."

"I already feel married," Ryan said with a shrug. "Honestly, we could go down to the courthouse and get married. It would be fine with me."

Mariah shot her beloved a look. "Your sister would kill us both. So would our mothers. Now, your dad and my dad might defend us but I can't promise that."

Ryan's relationship with his family had improved about a thousand percent in the last months. He understood there were things that his father simply couldn't say out loud, but that didn't mean that he didn't feel them. But a funny thing…now that Ryan didn't expect his parents to show much affection, they seemed to be trying to do just that. Last time they'd left Chicago,

Jack had given his son a hug. It was awkward but it was progress.

There was more talk about babies and weddings as they folded up and bagged the empty pizza boxes. They started working on Mariah's kitchen items and with so many hands it was done and organized in a few hours.

"It would have been faster if you didn't use shelf paper," Knox complained good-naturedly. "Is that a female thing? I've never used shelf paper. Am I missing out? Do I need shelf paper in my life?"

Shaw nodded solemnly. "You need shelf paper."

"And drawer organizers," Luke added with a laugh. "At least that's what my mother and sister said. I didn't argue. Just go with it."

Knox sighed dramatically. "I guess I need to get right on that then."

Chris popped open a can of soda. "I hate to bring the conversation down but I have to ask how it went."

They all knew what "it" was.

Two days ago, Sebastian Harrington had pled guilty to a single manslaughter charge in exchange for no jail time. He would, however, have ten years' probation and be required to do community service.

Ryan had flown back for the court date but Mariah stayed in Seattle since he only planned to be gone a few days. She needed to finish a commission and couldn't get away.

"He had to tell the whole story to the judge," Ryan replied. "It was exactly as he told me before."

The night the police had pulled Seb off of an airplane that was almost ready to taxi down the runway, he'd eventually talked to Ryan and told him everything. It was tragic and sad.

Seb was a senior in high school and he was actually the one gambling tons of money, drinking, and taking drugs. Since Seb didn't have access to his trust fund yet – he was under eighteen – Brad was covering his losses so Skip and Lilly wouldn't find out. The parents, if they noticed anything, would have simply put it down to Brad spending it on girlfriends and partying.

But Brad actually did leave the bar that night. Seb had snuck into the bar with a fake ID, wearing a hoodie that he'd pulled up to cover his face. He was afraid that Brad's friends would recognize him. He'd run up even more debts on cocaine and hookers and was afraid to tell his parents. He owed money and his loan sharks wanted it. Right away.

Consequently, Brad and Seb had traded clothes in the men's room. Brad had gone out the front door wearing Seb's hoodie over his face. Seb had gone out the bathroom window and waited at the construction site while Brad led the bookie who was trying to collect away from Seb.

When Brad lost the man looking for his brother, he doubled back and met Seb in the construction site. They argued, Brad wanting his younger brother to go to rehab and Seb saying that he wasn't that bad. He'd change and it would be okay. Brad wanted to tell their parents – or call the therapist that Brad had found named Aaron – and that's when it became physical. Brad threw a punch and then Seb threw one as well, but Brad knocked the younger brother on his back. Seb instinctively reached for a piece of pipe lying next to him and hit Brad on the side of the head, killing him.

Panicked and still under the influence of drugs and alcohol, Seb pushed Brad into a shallow hole and covered him in dirt. He then went back home and waited for the police to come arrest him. He was surprised when that didn't happen and he realized that everyone thought that Brad was in Hawaii. The construction crew poured concrete that week and by the time the family was looking for Brad he wasn't going to be easily found.

Seb went into rehab a few months later, his parents not aware of the extent of his issues. To make up for what he'd done, he tried to be the perfect son and husband, giving to charities and making a difference in his community.

As for Jack and Lilly, they didn't know what had transpired that night. If they had, they obviously wouldn't have brought Ryan in to investigate. It was only when Ryan said that Brad was a gambling addict that they had an inkling that Seb had somehow been involved. When Ryan left the couple, they'd dragged the truth out of their younger son.

Deciding they couldn't lose a second child, Skip had used his money and influential connections to send his son overseas where the long arm of the law hopefully wouldn't be able to touch him. When Ryan had shown up at the party asking to talk to Seb, Skip had realized that he had to stall, giving his son's flight a chance to take off.

"I can't imagine how the younger brother kept this to himself all of these years," Ella said. "It's just all so sad. And now his own dad has had to face charges, too."

Skip had been charged with assault for holding that knife to Mariah's throat, plus obstruction of justice. Months ago, he'd pled out and received probation and a hefty fine.

"They appear to have pulled together as a family," Ryan observed. "And I don't think that Seb is a danger to society."

"Do you believe his story?" Shaw asked quietly. "Do you believe it was an accident? Really and truly?"

"I've gone back and forth over that," Mariah confessed when Ryan didn't answer right away. "I want to believe Seb, and his story sounds credible. I sometimes wonder if it's my own cynicism that doubts him."

"Mine too," Shaw agreed. "But I'd want to believe him as well."

Rubbing his chin, Ryan finally answered. "I think I'm with Mariah on this one. I want to believe that Seb is telling the truth. I don't want to believe that a brother would kill another brother. If his parents can have faith in him, then I think that we should, too. We'll never be able to get Brad's side of the story."

"So your friend is finally resting in peace," Luke said. "Someone is answering for his death."

The conversation dwindled, and the group worked on a few more boxes. As the sun began to go down their friends went home, one by one, until it was just Ryan and Mariah. He flipped off the porch light as the last car drove away and locked the door.

Leaning against him, she pressed her head to his chest. She loved hearing his heart beating solidly under her cheek. It was somehow calming and exciting all at the same time.

"Are you tired?" Ryan asked. She'd been exhausted lately due to the pregnancy. "How about I run you a nice hot bath?"

They had a jetted tub in the master bath. It had been one of her requests when they were looking at real estate. She spent as much time as she could in it, knowing that in a few months it was going to take a crane to lift her out of it. She'd be taking showers for awhile.

"I'd love that. You're a pretty fantastic dad already. I think you're going to hit this parent stuff out of the park."

His arms slid around her middle, tugging her even closer. She could feel the heat of his body flush against hers. She'd never get tired of this. She'd been without him for so long.

I'm so grateful for a second chance.

"That's because I love you so much. And our baby. I want to make sure that you know how much every single day. This generation of the Beck family is going to change."

"Don't change too much. I love you just the way you are."

"I think we've both changed just enough."

Just enough. That's all they'd really needed.

A second chance at true love and a little bit of learning how to compromise.

Now they had their entire future spread out before them…together.

Thank you for reading! I hope you enjoyed Gilded Craving. There will be more stories in the Cowboy Justice Association: Serials and Stalkers series. Coming soon.

Thank you again for reading.

ABOUT THE AUTHOR

Olivia Jaymes is a wife, mother, lover of sexy romance and cozy mysteries, and caffeine addict. She lives with her husband, son, and two spoiled dogs in central Florida and spends her days typing on her computer with a canine on her lap.

She is currently working on a new cozy mystery series – *A Ravenmist Whodunit* – in addition to her other ongoing romance series.

Visit Olivia Jaymes at

www.OliviaJaymes.com

www.ingramcontent.com/pod-product-compliance
Lightning Source LLC
Chambersburg PA
CBHW030532270626
47155CB00024B/2788